微風輕拂白樺林。

林暄涵 著

Breeze Blowing through the Birch Forest

Written by Xuan-Han Lin

目次

PREFACE 序。

對我來說，成為藝術經紀人是命運的安排。而認識這些來自烏克蘭的藝術家，也亦然。只能說緣分將我們連接在一起，我們成了命運的共同體。

最初看到他們的藝術品時，深深地被他們的顏色和內涵所吸引，感覺他們的創作非常有特色。來往的過程中，漸漸地我對烏克蘭這個國家產生了好奇心，開始嘗試去了解他們的文化、歷史以及人文風情等。

這是一個有著深厚文化底蘊的國家，長期受到壓迫和統治，仍舊努力維護著自身的民族文化。雖然土地面積是歐洲第二大國，但人口僅約略為台灣的兩倍，貧富差異極大，中產階級人口的比例僅佔二成五左右。國內幾乎每一個城市都有一定規模的美術館和博物館，收藏著很多世界著名的名畫，還有許多培養美術人才的大學和專科學校，其中包含了國立基輔美術學院、國立哈爾科夫設計與藝術學院、國立利沃夫美術學院三所主要的國立美術學院，培養了眾多藝術的專業人才。

雖然烏克蘭大眾的文化素養普遍很高，也非常熱愛欣賞和收藏藝術品，但由於國家獨立時間不長，多數人的經濟收入水準偏低，因此購買能力非常有限，所以畫價與畫家的勞動付出懸殊很大。而且，近幾年國內缺乏真正高品質的專業畫廊和藝術市場，所以烏克蘭的藝術家們都盡量往海外發展以尋求出路，他們的作品得到了全世界公認的好評。

我感覺烏克蘭和台灣似乎從歷史進程的遭遇上講，命運上有所近似，但是台灣幸運的是中產階級的比例還算高，一般人民生活還算富足，也有比較長期的收藏藝術品的傳統和愛好。我之所以將幾位烏克蘭藝術家介紹到台灣，除了希望豐富台灣的藝術市場外，也希望將他們認真創作，儘管生活也許不盡人意，但卻仍舊孜孜不倦地追求藝術真諦的精神傳遞到台灣，將他們這些思想性極強和技巧十分高明、內涵極深的作品分享給大家。

弗拉基米爾是我很欣賞的藝術家，做事嚴謹，雖然話不多但充滿了幽默的想像力，他筆下的世界總是充滿了思想，但又很平易近人。羅曼是個積極的畫家，對於人生充滿了激情，更是個色彩高手。他畫的女人非常高雅自信，溫柔又有包容力。娜塔莎的作品充滿了設計感，裝飾性強且色彩鮮艷，更棒的是她的畫充滿了童話般的純真。亞歷克山大是個可愛的大男孩，喜歡十三、四世紀中古壁畫的單純潔淨感，所以他的畫作看了深感愜意，具有非同尋常的詩意。薩芬娜則是個令人驚奇的女孩，年紀非常輕但才華洋溢，我知道她即將成為頂尖的藝術家。

令人欣慰的是，藝術沒有國界的隔閡，沒有言語的障礙。因之，我能夠將我的感動傳遞給大家。我相信對於美的事物，應該是人人都有感受的能力。只要用真摯的雙眼和真誠的心靈去觀看、去感受，自然就能夠進入到烏克蘭畫家為我們創造的世界：一個從畫布上延伸出去的寬廣宇宙。這也是我所提倡的「美，沒有國界」的理念，我深信這就是藝術品非常重要的價值所在。

CHAPTER 1.

烏克蘭繪畫的過去和現在。

The Past and Now of Ukrainian Painting

1

2

烏克蘭，是一個遙遠的國度，在那片如畫的土地上，孕育了悠久的歷史和深厚的文化內涵，建立在這種人文薈萃之上的繪畫藝術，以其豐富的民族文化特徵和審美情趣在世界文化大花園中獨樹一幟。

她是歐洲除俄羅斯以外面積最大的國家，東與俄羅斯接壤，西與波蘭、斯洛伐克、匈牙利、羅馬尼亞、摩爾多瓦等諸國相連，南接黑海，北與白俄羅斯毗鄰。除了部分山地和高原，大部分是廣袤的平原。有許多河川流經各地，其中，最長的第聶伯河縱貫南北。全國的綠化覆蓋面積達百分之六十，是歐洲非常重要的糧倉，且擁有非常豐富的礦藏資源，同時擁有大片肥沃的黑土地，佔全世界黑土帶總面積的四成左右。擁有一百三十個民族，藝術傳統豐富多彩。

首都基輔機場外面是一片片淡鵝黃色的白樺林，在銀灰色厚重的雲層襯托下格外耀眼奪目，風徐徐拂過，發出如歌般的輕吟聲。市區裡到處是保護得很好的歐式古老建築和綠樹成蔭的整潔街道。傍晚漫步在第聶伯河畔的小樹林中，踏著柔軟的沙地，聆聽從遠處傳來的教堂鐘聲，腦裡會閃現出大文豪托爾斯泰（Leo Tolstoy,1828-1910)的巨著《復活》中所描寫的種種片段，這部不朽之作的許多情節正是以烏克蘭作為背景的。烏克蘭有著悠久的歷史，俄羅斯帝國是後來才建立在基輔公國的基礎之上的。她歷來飽受了多次外族和外國的入侵和佔領，曾被劃歸為俄羅斯，直到一九九一年才得以真正的獨立。

縱觀烏克蘭的文化，似乎與俄羅斯難以分別。其實，俄羅斯引以為榮的世界聞名巨匠如大文豪果戈理（Nikolai Vasilievich Gogol-Yanovski, 1809-1852），肖洛姆·阿萊漢姆(Sholom Alechem ,1859-1916)，大詩人畫家舍甫琴科（Taras Hryhorovych Shevchenko ,1814 - 1861），大畫家列賓(Ilya Efimovich Repin ,1844-1930)，庫茵芝(Arkhip Kuindzhi,1842-1898)，艾伊瓦佐夫斯基（Ivan

3

4

Konstantinovich Aivazovsky,1817-1900）， 女畫家齊內達
（Zinaida Serebriakova,1884-1967），現代大畫家雅勃隆斯
卡婭(Tatiana Yablonskaya,1917-2005)，大作曲家普羅高菲
夫（Sergei Sergeyevich Prokofiev,1891-1953），格里埃爾
（Reinhold Moritzevich Glière,1875-1956）等等都是從烏克蘭
走向世界的。他們的作品全都帶有著濃厚的烏克蘭情愫與
地域特色，在世界文化的頂尖隊列中佔據著不朽的地位。

烏克蘭有著深厚的文化底蘊，幾乎全民皆能歌善舞。人們
對藝術普遍有許多炙熱的愛好和高水準的鑒賞力，全國各
地擁有許多美術館和博物館，幾乎大多數屬於國立形制，
常年免費開放，不少世界聞名的畫作在其中永久陳列。休
假日，人們除了去音樂廳觀賞芭蕾舞劇，聆聽交響樂團演
出之外，還到美術館觀賞名畫和當代畫展。

談到她的繪畫史，自十世紀以來，烏克蘭繪畫主要是為教
會和宮廷服務的，受到神學的深刻影響，是為全宗教化。
十四世紀初，烏克蘭在希臘人的指導下製作了教堂壁畫和
聖像畫。這些具有平面構圖，單純明亮的色彩，及有力度
的線條和簡約概括輪廓的繪畫，成為烏克蘭早期美術的風
格及後來繪畫發展的源泉。之後，歐洲文藝復興運動和啓
蒙運動大大影響了烏克蘭美術，跟隨著西方化的改革運
動，烏克蘭美術開始走向歐洲化的道路；從國外聘請專家
傳授技法，派遣國內的藝術人才去歐洲各國學習。此時的
肖像畫得到很大的發展，寫實人物技法延續了聖像畫的技
法，功力深厚，且開始重視科學性如透視、質感和人物解
剖結構關係的運用。

1. 聖史路德｜聖像畫｜11-12 世紀｜烏克蘭沃倫州聖像畫博物館
2. 列賓｜托爾斯泰肖像｜207x73cm｜1901｜國立俄羅斯美術館藏
3. 列賓｜烏克蘭農婦｜1875｜私人收藏
4. 列賓｜圍籬旁的烏克蘭女孩｜1876｜白俄羅斯明斯克美術館藏

5

6

十七至十八世紀歐洲啓蒙運動的民主化趨勢深刻地影響到烏克蘭的藝術，其畫家們深受自由平等及理性思想的感染，開始重視藝術的教育功能與社會功能，要求藝術履行道德職責，參與社會改造任務。他們創作了許多批判和抨擊農奴制度的、以及抗擊外來統治的作品，並將注意力凝聚在中下層百姓和鄉村的田園風光之中，以此抒發久已壓抑的愛國情懷。

十八世紀中後期，俄羅斯及烏克蘭陸續開辦了多所美術學院，有系統並科學地培養專業人才，使得其美術事業得到健康繁榮的進步，為今日的烏克蘭美術躋身於世界美術的巔峰打下了堅實的基礎。

十九世紀，西方的美學思想在俄羅斯以及烏克蘭民主主義者那裡得到發展。美術創作逐步擺脫了宗教與政府的約束，積極面向生活，反對純藝術的主張，極力提倡現實主義，並吸收了古典主義和浪漫主義的精華，因之形成了強大的批判現實主義風潮。一八七〇年俄羅斯成立的《巡回展覽畫派》就是其中的核心組織。這是一個以現實主義為創作目標的進步美術家組織，烏克蘭或原籍烏克蘭的畫家也受到了極大的影響並積極參與。他們遵從「美就是生活」的創作原則，從民主自由的立場出發，描繪廣大民眾的生活和歷史，以及勞動的美感，借此表達民眾要求解脫苦難的願望，揭露和批判專制制度。這個畫派的創作思想和創作方法與學院派相對立，取得了輝煌的成就，成功地將民主主義與現實主義相結合，為後來的社會主義的美術發展奠定了基礎。

二十世紀初，轟動世界的《巡迴展覽畫派》經過五十三年後，逐漸失去了昔日畫壇盟主的位置和光芒。畫派內部發生了分歧，部分畫家對以往的創作經歷進行了反思。他們認為藝術家應當具有自己的個性，在西歐現代主義思潮的憧憬下，極力主張創作自由而不受任何意識形態和權力影響，注重藝術語彙的獨立性和純粹的形式與技巧。他們吸取現代藝術的方法，並信奉古典主義的唯美樣式，在接納現實主義的影響之外，在藝術創作上有許多創新與變革。

7

他們將西方的現代手法運用到舞台美術、民間美術、工業設計、書籍插圖裝幀、雕塑等多種領域。他們是藝術的探索者、革新者和開拓者，是前衛藝術的先驅。這個時期的主要代表組織就是《藝術世界》。爾後，俄國十月革命風潮席捲全國，自然，烏克蘭也在其中。由於政見的不同，一些著名的先鋒藝術家和著名畫家擔心受到批判和迫害，因此流亡到國外，成為歐洲現代主義運動的核心人物。

8

5. 舍甫琴科｜農家｜60x72.5 cm｜1843｜塔拉斯‧舍甫琴科國立美術館藏
6. 舍甫琴科｜卡特琳娜詩集插畫｜93x72.3 cm｜1842｜塔拉斯‧舍甫琴科國立美術館藏
7. 庫茵芝｜第聶伯河上的月夜｜105x144 cm｜1880｜莫斯科特列恰柯夫美術館藏
8. 庫茵芝｜白樺林｜97x181cm｜1881｜莫斯科特列恰柯夫美術館藏

9

10

這些人當中有不少是從烏克蘭逃過鄰國而到達西方世界的,至於留在國內的畫家則天真的以為革命會帶給藝術創作更大的自由,除了熱情迎合政府對「藝術為政治服務」的要求之外,也出現了裝飾風格和照相寫實的作品。但是隨著蘇聯政府,尤其是史達林時期對非主流的現代藝術進行無情打壓,因此,受到當局提倡和扶植的「社會主義的現實主義」繪畫迅速的成長,當然,其中也不乏一些畫家出於本能和良心所創作的較為貼近生活的優秀作品。

二十世紀七〇年代左右,政府開始施行半開放的文藝政策,非主流的作品得到發展,出現了一些新的風格和流派,以及反現實主義的傾向。畫家們的作品先是嘲諷否定當局的作為,後來發展到尖銳批評制度的地步。八〇年代末期,蘇聯面臨解體的危機,政府對藝術的掌控已力不從心,乾脆改變初衷,轉而支持非官方藝術。到了蘇聯解體的最後階段時,官方已經無力關注藝術創作,從此,美術創作的空間變得自由廣闊,不僅內容廣泛,且形式更加豐富多彩,呈現了多元化的格局。

11

12

從前蘇聯獨立出來之後，烏克蘭畫家是自由開放的；他們的前輩同行經過了藝術反叛、創新、勝利與失敗的過程，得以延續到今天。年輕的一代從思想上和繪畫觀念上迅速同歐洲先進國家接軌，他們除了繼承先輩的傳統，積極關心社會，盡力表現大眾的感受和痛楚之外，更對歷史變遷、社會變化、生活、情感，以及現實體驗和領悟進行了更深刻的思索，並大膽地評擊時弊，同時，還採用更多的本國民間藝術的稚拙手法以強調自身的創作個性，並將其轉化為創作的原初動機。他們充分運用紮實的文化和技巧功底，開闊眼界並廣泛吸收世界各國的藝術精髓，且融合自身民族的藝術精華，探索了更有個性、更深刻的表現方式。因而，當今的烏克蘭畫家更自然地融入了二十一世紀的時代氣息，使烏克蘭文化注入了新鮮的血液，得以向前快速地發展。

9. 艾伊瓦佐夫斯基｜黑海｜208x144 cm｜1881｜莫斯科特列恰柯夫美術館藏
10. 艾伊瓦佐夫斯基｜九級浪濤｜221x332 cm｜1850｜國立俄羅斯美術館藏
11. 齊內達｜收成｜71.5x88.5 cm｜1915｜烏克蘭奧德賽國家美術館藏
12. 齊內達｜紙牌屋｜60x74 cm｜1919｜私人收藏
13. 齊內達｜少女｜60x74 cm｜1935｜私人收藏

14

15

16

如今，我們甚至可以說：烏克蘭的繪畫發展歷程就是東歐當代繪畫發展的縮影，在西方藝術衝擊的大背景下，烏克蘭在全球化的藝術浪潮中不僅能融入其中，而且彰顯出自身的民族文化特色，屹立在世界藝術之林。在今天的國際藝術市場上，烏克蘭藝術家活躍其間，成績令人矚目，其作品被許多國家的美術館、博物館等機構收藏，這些都讓人看到烏克蘭繪畫藝術正在不斷地發展茁壯，成為世界藝術中的一支奇葩。

14. 雅勃隆斯卡婭｜收成｜201x340 cm｜1949｜莫斯科特列恰柯夫美術館藏
15. 雅勃隆斯卡婭｜農婦｜1966｜私人收藏
16. 雅勃隆斯卡婭｜編織者｜94x85 cm｜1958｜私人收藏
17. 雅勃隆斯卡婭｜收割黃瓜｜150x180 cm｜1966｜私人收藏

(右圖)相遇｜油彩‧畫布
(Right) Encounter ｜ Oil on Canvas ｜ 52x39cm ｜ 2009

CHAPTER 2

人間喜劇。

－弗拉基米爾 *Volodymyr Neskoromnyi*

弗拉基米爾是一位喜歡思索並將自己的見解付諸其作品的藝術家，對社會、對人生都有他獨特的看法。他的思想開放自由，想像力豐富。他筆下的世界就像是一幅幅巴爾扎克筆下的人間喜劇畫作。

列賓｜查布羅什人給蘇丹王寫信
358x203cm｜1880-1891｜國立俄羅斯美術館藏

他出生於烏克蘭查布羅什地區。他的先輩，同樣出生於烏克蘭的俄羅斯大畫家伊利亞‧列賓在他的巨作《查布羅什人給蘇丹王寫信》中，十分生動精辟地描繪出了查布羅什人倔強而詼諧，驍勇而樸實的形象。這對我們瞭解和認識弗拉基米爾個人的品性以及繪畫風格會有著參考的意義。無論是選擇大型歷史題材還是敘事小品的創作，如宗教神話或是異國見聞，以及日常生活描述，他都採用調侃風趣的語彙來表現。

弗拉基米爾的畫看似十分諧趣，其實卻充滿了哲理和智慧。他將自己對人生和對時局的看法潛藏於其作品之中。每一幅畫作都滲透了他深刻敏銳的思想。當我們被他的畫作感染得捧腹大笑的同時，也會即刻去探究畫內深遠的寓意。他為觀眾設置了一座座很特別的舞台，按照自己的需要，隨意組合人物角色，主觀設定造型，並讓這些角色任意穿越，不受時空的限制。他畫筆下幾乎都是平民百姓和生活，但他們的表情和行為又是十分滑稽可笑的。畫家用極其嚴肅的創作態度在為觀眾講述荒誕的故事，因而，他的作品雖然採用了傳統寫實手法，但應當歸宿於當代<黑色幽默>的創作範疇。

因為受過長期嚴謹的專業訓練，所以他的畫看似輕鬆隨意，其實造型十分紮實嚴謹。尤其在把握整體構圖方面，人物景物相互呼應協調，虛實得當，空間深遠。筆觸輕重交錯，結構非常準確。在色彩運用上，注重全局色調的統一，局部冷暖的微妙對比。更為寶貴的是，他非常強調畫面的光感以及顏色隨情緒需要的變化，使得他的畫幅雖不大，卻能具有大型繪畫的特質，也即大氣磅礴的感覺。

我非常欣賞他，因為他的作品將不起眼的平凡生活，轉換為一部有價值的社會風俗史。而且，他不是機械地再現生活，反而著重表現自身對世俗的主觀理解，並透過高明的技巧和優雅的色調，創造出一種表現力極強的藝術形式。他的繪畫形式充滿了文學的敘事性，樸實的畫面構成裡包含著深刻的思想，達到了一般當代藝術作品所未能達到的更高境界。

這張作品是畫家十多年前的創作，是《聖經》中最典型的內容，耶穌基督從十字架上被放下來，聖母瑪利亞與眾人無限悲痛。上面一聯表現的是耶穌基督升天，小天使在一旁精心呵護著。橙紅的色調統一著整幅畫面，更顯得莊重悲壯。每個人物的動態和表情都經過了精心的刻畫，十分生動。畫風細膩而大氣，觀眾彷彿聽到了撕心裂肺的呼號和哭聲。飛翔的天使和耶穌基督寓意著解脫和希望。畫的右方有一位年輕人扶著殘缺的木梯，這種表現手法是作者的處理，用以同經典的同類題材作品區別。整幅畫作充滿了古代壁畫因時間久遠而斑駁脫落的效果。

哀悼耶穌｜油彩・畫布　　Lamentation｜Oil on Canvas｜24x100cm(up)74x100cm(bottom)｜1999

這是從古至今被畫家們重複了無數次的題材。畫家運用壁畫的構圖，以自己獨有的方式來進行創作。前景刻畫了美麗的歐羅巴坐在宙斯化成的公牛身上，但是公牛被枷鎖架上，有農夫在強迫拉著，後頭還有兩位農夫在用棍子趕牛，甚至還有人推牛。一位戴墨鏡的老闆模樣的人指揮著這一切混亂。此公牛已不是原來意義的公牛！當今歐盟成了強勢，一些中小國家不得已都順應大潮，爭相加入歐盟，但卻同時失去了自己的個性和尊嚴。從前的歐羅巴是自願坐上公牛，但今日卻成了經濟資本的奴隸被迫上陣。畫家透過這幅畫對時代做出嘲諷，後面幾位騎牛的女孩正好補充了大家都爭相仿效的時尚風氣。

(左圖)誘拐歐羅巴－I｜油彩・畫布
(Left) Abduction of Europe - I｜Oil on Canvas｜90x140cm｜2002

(右圖)誘拐歐羅巴－II｜油彩・畫布
(Right) Abduction of Europe - II｜Oil on Canvas｜33x46cm｜2009

遊戲｜油彩‧畫布
Game｜Oil on Canvas｜70x100cm｜2010

這幅作品採用魔幻現實的手法，表現了人生如遊戲的戲
劇性主題。畫中散落著幾組進行日常生活的中世紀打扮
的人群，有老有小、有男有女、有站有坐、有運動有靜
止，看似不相干，但被統一安排在典型的烏克蘭的風景
之中。前面主體人物是一位提著小棍的女孩。小棍一頭
繫著紙團，是為了戲弄貓咪的。還有一位男孩被黑布包
著雙眼，提著關鳥的木籠，麻木地坐在那裡。他們放任
迫不及待的小貓和小狗在那裡騷動，好似等待著觀眾發
出開始遊戲的號令。右下方擱置著一個人偶胸像以強調
畫面的戲劇效果，意味著畫家利用其作品直接與觀眾產
生精神上的交流和互動。

觀眾在欣賞畫作的時候會強烈地感受到所有的人和物都
處在一個大舞台之中，使得我們好像在觀看一場喜劇或
是一幕輕歌劇。畫家巧妙地運用諧趣的造型語言來表達
非常嚴肅的思想，即人生本來就是一個大舞台，使得該
畫作具有了極其深刻的內涵。畫面的色彩對比處理跳躍
又協和，人物造型生動詼諧，可以看出畫家具有高超的
藝術和哲學修養。

《睡眠》描寫的是瑪利亞在逃往埃及途中休息的場景，人們在吹著牧笛號角，安慰著因疲倦緊張而哭泣的瑪利亞，聖子安詳地睡著了。連烏鴉和小狗也在安慰他們。

驢子伸長了脖子在傾聽著樂曲，累了的小丑拿下面具坐著。傍晚的背景有幾間典型的烏克蘭農舍，一位戴著棉帽的現代清掃工正在打掃著，預示一天的結束。前景打瞌睡的現代女人和裝模作樣看報紙的光頭孩子將觀眾拉回到當下的時光。這是畫家又一幅時空穿越的傑作，美妙的色彩和造型引領觀眾穿梭於不同的時空之中。

睡眠
油彩・畫布

Sleep
Oil on Canvas
60x120cm
2010

畫面前方這位大鬍子拿書的人也許是歷史學家，手裡捧著聖經。小男孩代表天真的當代兒童坐在石頭上面，好奇的看著發生的一切，他也許代表了畫家本人。驢子前面還有一位古代學者提著錐型測量儀在做測量定位。背景有誇張的城牆和懸在天空的金字塔意味著抵達目的地了。人們在宣傳和丈量土地，讓聖母子落戶。吹號角農婦和打小旗幟的以色列聖徒正在宣佈聖母子的到來。畫面以斑剝脫落的藍色塊處理方式來模擬古代壁畫的效果。畫作寓意著當今同古代一樣，真理和善良被世俗四處驅逐。

我認為，弗拉基米爾的作品，畫出了他本人很有深度的思想，不是畫所見而是畫所想，價值非凡。

逃往埃及｜油彩・畫布
Escape to Egypt｜Oil on Canvas｜70x100cm｜2012

小型運動-III｜油彩・畫布
Small Sports -III｜Oil on Canvas｜80x100cm｜2012

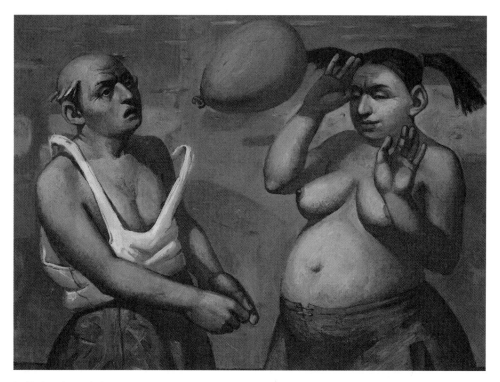

打排球｜油彩·畫布
Volley Ball ｜Oil on Canvas｜80x100cm｜2009

小型運動系列是畫家借用一對平凡的夫婦進行各種小型競技的幽默描繪，來表達家庭及人與人之間常有的衝突、矛盾和較勁。在畫家看來這些情景其實非常滑稽，而且可笑又可愛。觀眾們在這些親切可笑的畫作面前能發出會心的笑聲，一切煩惱都化解得煙消雲散。看似小競技，其實包含了人生的大哲理。這就是弗拉基米爾的高明之處。

你看，《拳擊》捨不得拳頭，反用頭來互頂；《小型運動 - I 》中，為了爭得拔河比賽的一點點距離，兩人在那裡囉嗦爭論得喋喋不休；《打排球》實際上是打氣球，軟軟的飄來飄去還認真的不得了；《小型運動 - II 》中，划船的兩人並不協調各懷心思，只是風不識趣地將船帆鼓起，好像幫了男人，烏鴉帶著疑惑的表情在看著這場喜劇；《小型運動 - III 》中，紅色的著名烏克蘭大肥豬狂奔著，全然不顧裸體女選手就將被顛下來。這些畫中的人物表情雖然滑稽但都十分嚴肅，更加令人捧腹大笑。畫作的技巧性和藝術性非常高，構圖飽滿，色彩協調，十分耐看。

拳擊 | 油彩・畫布
Boxing | Oil on Canvas | 80x100cm | 2009

The painter applies one average couple to the small sport series to carry out various competitions through humorous depiction, whereas common conflicts, contradictions and rivalries between families and people are depicted. These scenes in fact all look ridiculous, funny and lovely to the painter. The viewers will make a knowing laughter in front of these friendly and funny paintings while all worries will be dissolved completely. The genius of the artist is to hide some important philosophy from these small competitions.

As you can see, the boxers do not use their fists but their heads. In order to advance each other with a little distance from the tug of war, two people are long-winded and quarreling nonstop.Playing balloon to replace volleyball and the soft balloon simply floats all over as if engaged in serious competition. The two people boating do not look coordinated and are thinking differently. However the wind unknowingly blows up the sail to help the man while the crow looks down this comedy with a suspicious expression. The red famous Ukraine pig bolted and completely ignores the nude female athlete who is flipped down. Although all the characters hold ridiculous expression, they are quite serious and that makes them look even funnier. The paintings come with high artistic techniques with full composition, coordinating colors and high engagement.

小型運動-II｜油彩‧畫布
Small Sports -II｜Oil on Canvas｜80x120cm｜2010

我喜歡幽默的表現手法，
主要喜歡將一般市井小民的生活，
透過樸實的技法表達出來，
讓觀者快樂愉悅的理解到我的訴求。

- 弗拉基米爾自述 -

小型運動-I｜油彩·畫布
Small Sports -I｜Oil on Canvas｜60x100cm｜2009

這些作品是畫家到中國講學時畫的(P36-P41)。他多次到中國，利用平時空閒時間到處觀察民間生活，拍了許多照片，畫了許多寫生。他並沒有原封不動的照搬現實情境，而是排除現實的干擾，畫出自己的感受。他表述的是弗拉基米爾看中國！他只重視自己的第一感覺，而不去機械的模仿現實，盡可能同照相術區分開來。我認為真正的畫家應該是像這樣子創作的，而這也是藝術創造和新聞攝影的區別點。

《農婦》就是畫家的印象之作；一位露著大肚皮的中國農婦挑著籮筐在塵土飛揚的小城鎮角落站立著，穿著另類的西式披肩和條紋褲，自信又有幾分得意。這就是典型的外國人眼中的當代中國人形象。背景有幾個都市人在行走，還有表示南方的棕櫚樹。令人想起西班牙大畫家何塞.德里貝拉筆下的跛足少年和中國作家魯迅小說中的阿Q。

(左圖)農婦｜油彩·畫布
(Left) Peasant Woman｜Oil on Canvas｜45x40cm｜2010

(右圖)黃昏禮服｜油彩·畫布
(Right) Evening Dress｜Oil on Canvas｜45x60cm｜2008

中國的大排檔，在畫家心目中是有趣又稀奇的；高談闊論的婦女，內衣拉
到腹上的男士，他們大口的吸煙，啤酒一瓶接一瓶地喝。這在中國是到處
可見的景象，十分世俗卻也非常真實。右方婦女面戴時髦的太陽眼鏡，腳
懸在空中故作優雅，牽著一隻看來很可笑的小貓，誇張地表現出女性矯揉
做作又滑稽可笑的樣態。這張畫不是靜態的，是帶著嘈雜聲音，幽默且真
實，而且充滿了動感的人生片段。

(左圖)世紀演說｜油彩‧畫布
(Left) Speech of Century ｜Oil on Canvas｜61x72cm｜2009

(右圖)農村主題｜油彩‧畫布
(Right) Rural Motive｜Oil on Canvas｜55x40cm｜2012

這是弗拉基米爾眼中的當代世俗情景；民工和民女、人力板車、牛仔褲、涼鞋……

右下方的看板上的文字，寫了：「世界之旅」，以及「塞浦路斯」、「希臘」、「馬耳他」等與烏克蘭南部克里米亞接壤的西方國家。手持中國式雨傘的少女，穿著高雅的西式風衣配上尚未習慣的高跟鞋，她們嚮往著嫁到外國，憧憬更美好的人生。這樣混搭的裝扮，以及婦人在紅綠交通燈下不知所措的動態，調侃式地表現出不協調美感的趣味性。

(左圖)轉變│油彩·畫布
(Left) Transition │ Oil on Canvas │ 45x30cm │ 2010

(右圖)戰士│油彩·畫布
(Right) Warrior │ Oil on Canvas │ 40x45cm │ 2012

神話中的亞馬遜女戰士騎在馬上的英姿,是畫家所感受到的現代女性特質:勇敢、積極、自信。這是一種紀念碑式的構圖,強調出現代女性的英雄氣概。整幅作品以雅緻且高級的藍灰色為主調,並巧妙閃爍其對比顏色的黃色。下方鋪陳日常生活的人們,更加突顯出主體的特質,拉近了神話與現實的距離,使觀眾的思維得以從古代到今日自然地穿越,再度表現出畫家的調侃性格。

在月光下，中國的亞當夏娃站立在泥土圍牆前面，夏娃拿著摘到手的蘋果低著頭，亞當的臉上似乎有幾分焦慮，啓明星在他們頭頂上照耀著，黎明到來時，將有何種命運在等待著他們呢？

The Chinese Adam and Eve are standing in front of the mud wall beneath the moonlight. Eve lowers her head while holding the freshly picked apple and Adam seems to be anxious. The stars are sparkling above them and we don't know what kind of fate is waiting for them by the dawn.

亞當與夏娃｜油彩・畫布
Adam and Eve｜Oil on Canvas｜60x53cm｜2010

畫中的小型競技反映出人生的大舞台
OLEG KOVAL

藝術評論家／國立哈爾科夫設計與藝術學院教師

我要指出的是，這些在畫布上表現的多種樣式的小型運動綜合起來就是一個人生的大舞台。我並不是想要貶低繪畫存在於生活中的重要性，更不是要輕視弗拉基米爾的藝術創作，而是要強調弗拉基米爾用繪畫手段來表現人生的追求宗旨，並且巧妙地在繪畫的平面上借用人物的形象來表達運動和娛樂的行為，這是一種非常特殊的表現手段。

這位來自哈爾科夫的藝術家，別開生面地創造了上述怪誕的遊戲造型，他在作品中刻意摒棄誇張奇特的造型，而另闢新徑。二十至二十一世紀的藝術趨勢是摒棄以往傳統寫實的程式化創作思想模式，從這種模式之外去尋求靈感，並加以發揮，意旨加強作品的藝術性，也就是要更廣泛地從各個側面來創造特定的多風格的圖像表現形式。

弗拉基米爾熟練地揉合了跨學科的多個主題，製作出多樣化的造型，並且沒有損壞他原初希望講述的故事主題，以及他所完成的敘事性圖畫。他的畫面是形式、氣氛和手法等繪畫語彙的成功結合體。他獨特的繪畫語言是二十一世紀的後現代主義的表現手法，並且是結合了比較傾向保守繪畫手段的傳統主義，以及強調情感的風俗畫之後所融合的形式。他的繪畫，猶如畫布上正進行小型競技的男人女人們般，是不需要事先去特別將其繪畫的結構或圖像空間歸納成某種類型的，觀眾可以輕鬆地進行解讀。

任何想要進入弗拉基米爾的藝術境界裡的人，首先會被他所創造出來的寬闊的遠景造型，以及結實地刻劃出來的帶有後巴洛克時期造型和個性的人物、紀念碑式的穩定的平面造型等等所震撼，這些要素在厚重的肌理和清晰的二次元空間上更加被突顯深化出來。同時，弗拉基米爾在其獨創的穩重畫面上創造出了具有主觀意識的純正構圖，這是他堅實的功夫和圖像語彙的表現。

弗拉基米爾充滿了詩意的才華，而且對於繪畫的典型主體賦予了深刻的創意和微妙的感知能力。他非常擅長於建立自己的繪畫語境，並且能夠熟練地完成對當代文化的轉譯。同時，因為他優秀的繪畫才能，所以能夠在他所創作的顏色系統中，將一些相互對比的誇張色彩實施有機地組合，但整體卻又看來是統一的色調，並且建構出一個完整的敘事性圖像。

圖像的微妙詩感和複雜情緒，逐漸地被顏色的連續性淡化，而且被詮釋到各個複雜的主題和多元的造型內；他們被帶入圖像的洪流中，而且這些造型和神話的主題親密地融入到圖像內。這些詩意的表現，看得出來具備了古典學院派的影子，但又並非刻意地在他的創作緣起和作品完成時顯現出來。弗拉基米爾試圖利用大膽的造型和實驗性的視覺表現，將觀者帶回古典繪畫中那種率真無邪的境界。其作品中，形狀的感覺、空間和色彩的韻律感、微妙的顏色層次感、主題的可讀性，以及穩重潔淨的構圖都清晰地表達了他的想法。此外，他所使用的顏色，刻意概括簡化的人物造型、構圖、媒材，也都完美地融合在其作品裡。弗拉基米爾繪畫的獨創性，可以說是來自於他巧妙地結合古典和當代藝術的能力。

我們無法將他歸類為憂鬱的夢幻大師，但是在他的作品《黃昏禮服》、《世紀演講》、《熟悉的曲調》和《轉變》裡，我們注意到畫中人物靜止的表情在畫面上形成緩慢移動的片段，企圖形塑出獨特的造型外同時保有敏感的敘事性主題的氛圍。如畫的自我陶醉的表情不僅表達出各個生活流派的場景，同時也恰巧將科技時代的新的田園風情，而且也是一種宗教情懷的、虛無的習慣性理想化，將弗拉基米爾的內在創意準確的建構出來，成為極佳的視覺效果。

在《亞當和夏娃》和《哀悼耶穌》中，宗教主題化身為生活的場景，其動機幻化為風格造型，人物成為英雄，不是理想中的宗教性質的，而是真實的人生。人性化的故事情節，色彩和佈光成功的分配好各個情節，組合成主題明確的圖像空間。觀者得以被這強烈的手段帶入對主題的閱讀，同時融入到畫面所帶來的寧靜的歡愉之中。《亞當和夏娃》採用了一種接近象形文字般的表意手法，畫家創造出一個揭示了情感心理的幻境，借用了大眾皆知的主題，採用了大刀闊斧的筆觸，但並沒有將畫面變成厚塗，而是產生了類似壁畫技巧的感覺。祖先被天堂拒絕了，這樣的傳說故事常常會讓孩子傻眼，但是他們還是得堅持去抗爭。勇敢的夏娃，在被人生中的蘋果樹戲弄過後，竟然還是很快的就忘記傷痛，她的熱情促使她快速地在赤裸的身上披上禦寒的外衣，繼續引導著她那無知困惑且沒有經驗的小男孩似的丈夫。

然而，弗拉基米爾並不滿足於僅僅在牆壁前面放置這些粗壯的赤裸身軀，他將這些身軀做為象徵，建構了強力的連結——將原罪隱喻到空間和時間轉換的背景下。躲藏在視覺後面的樹的生命，還有幾乎看不見的通往天堂的大門，委婉地暗示出主題的緣由：所謂的「天真」對人類來說就好像看見了一個奇蹟，由於這個奇蹟而張開著嘴，擺著輕鬆的姿勢。對這張畫的主角們，或是對觀者來說，最重要的就是要用雙腳踏穩實地，迎接下個生命的誕生！

《哀悼耶穌》的戲劇性主題深化了圖畫的意象，加強了給予觀者的視覺衝擊力。作者預先設定並安排的構圖，如處在半圓弧形中的基督與下半部分的聖母及眾人有著不同的情緒和因之產生的不同的動態，就好像達文西在他的《最後的晚餐》中，描繪聖徒對待耶穌的語彙一樣，他捕捉到了不同特性的聖徒的個人反應。而弗拉基米爾在他自己的「聖母憐子圖」中，呈現了他自我的獨特的感情色彩以及對於悲痛的各種心理情緒的深刻描繪。另外，他塑造的耶穌形象與高更作品的平面造型類似，同時也是採用將顏料平塗的方式，僅僅勾勒出形體的輪廓，純粹依賴微妙的處理背景所產生的空間進行與主題相連接，以達到畫面具有強烈的節奏感，似乎凝固靜止的人物位置經營、扇形數字的字符位置安排、紅色的大面積渲染，種種這些手法巧妙地將原本嚴肅主題的繁複關係輕鬆地闡釋了。然而，即便弗拉基米爾採用了上述的圖像處理手段，我們仍然可以看出他意欲將平面的繪畫體現成為真實的生活，向真實靠攏，進而描繪出更顯明的情緒構造，而且基本上是有機的、大眾熟悉的、普遍的情緒，不是誇大的、做作的悲哀和苦楚。

弗拉基米爾及早就確立了自己的風格走向，成為一個捕捉日常生活場景的高手，他所描繪的不是表象的風景，而是內在的情緒。在烏克蘭，藝術總是陷入新巴洛克風格的趨勢中，而弗拉基米爾在創作群像或個人肖像的時候，特別注重必須包含精神的表達、人物的個性化，以及人物所處的社會位置的定位，追求平衡協調和精簡的造型構圖，因而在哈爾科夫成為了一個特別的畫家。

畫家的創作是給觀眾欣賞的，但同時渴望觀者能夠積極的進入和參與到圖畫的合奏中來，弗拉基米爾讓我們感受到構圖上色彩和造型的平衡感，他的作品具有著獨特的造型以及繪畫空間。這個空間成功地展現在觀眾面前，沒有任何的語彙和觀念不通的障礙阻擾。他運用這樣的手法將主題和作者的主觀意圖，以一般人能接受的視覺狀態明確地奉送給觀眾，觀者不再僅僅是被動的觀看，而是確實地去體驗了。

《小型運動》系列作品，透過形象的透視處理，嚴謹的對稱構圖，以及前景巧妙的安排，使得作品具有很奇特的視覺張力。弗拉基米爾賦予畫中的人物一些假設的運動行為，這些虛構的運動場景，虜獲了作為旁觀者的觀眾的視線，原來這是另一種生活比喻的路徑，同時也是戲劇性地比喻日常嚴苛的男女關係。畫面雖然安排明亮，卻都是非常平凡的大眾場景，主體人物處於同一平面中，但卻有著不安定的空間邊界處理。人物造型雖然是運動著的，但卻總是帶有一種疏離的動態感，這點和林布蘭的作品《杜爾博士的解剖學課》剛好相反；在林布蘭的作品裡，認真觀察杜爾博士解剖的八個人物，每人都積極的參與著這場視覺的事件，他們在畫作中擔當各自角色，都具有獨特的位置和給觀眾的視覺起到引導的作用。而弗拉基米爾所描繪的已婚的夫妻透過各種運動：如划船、拳擊、打排球和拔河等，用一句話來說，就是他使畫中的主角個體在作品的空間裡有身體的連接和接觸，但實質內心卻是矛盾重重。從人物動作設計來看，畫家似乎想表達：在現實生活之中確實存在著競爭性，這些人物直白的造型開啓了情緒的變異，從吶喊到沈默，從對立到跨越。我們可以從中觀察到人類心理特徵的複雜層次變化。

弗拉基米爾的肖像畫，主角都是自我滿足的，和馬奈的《吹短笛的男孩》相近，同時這也是畫家接受了後現代和後古典現代主義的表現手段。大體來說，他使用了自然天真、沈默的圖像語言來回應了新現代主義。仔細觀察《轉變》和《農婦》，強烈的民族色彩和自然普遍的主題，這些人物肖像的特色就是跳離了風格和主題的動機。整體的重點在於其形體；圓滾滾的農婦好像是在某個真實的地方生長起來的，但其實這個地方不過是個虛擬的位置，作家渴望揭示人體劃分比例的幾何構型規律。而《轉變》的女孩，是身處在一個似曾相識，但又非常寬廣的空間。她好像很自戀，但沒有暗示出任何意圖。事實上，女孩並非注視在她的外套或水坑上，而是小心翼翼地避免跨出畫的框架，因之，這幅畫將焦慮的日常生活場景轉換為一個真正的視覺作品。

我們正是如此端視弗拉基米爾的繪畫！在不破壞繪畫法則的原則上，這位藝術家致力追求將幻想化成真實，我覺得他已經成功的達成這個理想了。

CHAPTER 3.

流動的島嶼。

－羅曼 *Roman Nogin*

咖啡廳裡的女子們 - VI 《女人的對話》系列｜油彩‧畫布
The Ladies in Café - VI "Women Talk" series｜Oil on Canvas｜70x90cm｜2010

這是對一首熱情洋溢的爵士樂曲的闡釋。黑白兩位女孩被樂曲陶醉，正扭動著身軀起舞，咖啡廳裡擬人化的物件也似乎受到了感染在顫動著，鮮花盛放，布幔飄舞，一切都被美妙的音樂熏陶得充滿了無盡的活力。

This is the expounding of passionate jazz music, whereas the black and white girls are intoxicated in the music, moving their bodies to dance. The personated objects in the café seem to have affected and are trembling. The blooming flowers and the dance are filled with infinite vitality by the nourishment of the wonderful music.

(左圖) 咖啡廳裡的女子們-V《女人的對話》系列｜油彩‧畫布
(Left) The Ladies in Café - V "Women Talk" series｜Oil on Canvas｜70x50cm｜2010

(右圖) 咖啡廳裡的女子們-I《女人的對話》系列｜油彩‧畫布
(Right) The Ladies in Café - I "Women Talk" series｜Oil on Canvas｜61x92cm｜2009

羅曼是一位很認真的年輕藝術家，他的畫充滿了活力和激情。他的《女人的對話》系列使用的
是濃郁鮮艷的對比色彩，變形誇張甚至扭曲的造型，不規則的構圖，強調的是熱情的爵士樂的
感覺，以及隨著這音樂而來的舞蹈的活力。我們可以從他的作品聽到薩克斯和單簧管的吹奏、
大提琴的彈跳聲，還有踢踏的舞步聲，看到因極其投入而扭動身軀的演奏家和魅力四射的舞蹈
女郎。

咖啡廳裡的女子們-II《女人的對話》系列｜油彩・畫布
The Ladies in Café - II "Women Talk" series｜Oil on Canvas｜61x92cm｜2010

Roman is a serious and young artist, whose paintings are full of vigor and
passion. His " Women Talk " series are applied with strong and bright
contrasting colors that are deformed with exaggeration and even distortion.
The irregular composition emphasizes on the perception of passionate jazz
music as well as the vigor that accompanies this music. We can hear the
performance of saxophone and clarinet, the playing of cello, and the sound of
tap dance. The performers and the charming female dancers are moving their
body due to high devotion.

咖啡廳裡的女子們-III《女人的對話》系列│油彩·畫布
The Ladies in Café - III "Women Talk" series │Oil on Canvas│70x90cm│2010

介於具象與抽象之中

OLEG KOVAL

藝術評論家／國立哈爾科夫設計與藝術學院教師

二十世紀初，俄國的藝術家菲洛諾夫(Pavel Nikolaevitch Filonov)於1911-1913年間完成的作品，強調了「純粹表現形式」的前衛觀念。這個概念是講求作者在藝術創作的過程中，將所描寫的對象分解為各自獨立的許多部分，然後按照作者主觀的感受和意願，進一步孤立的表現和處理。一方面要清楚的表達每個基本的細節，另一方面又保持著畫面的高度完整性。這種透過解構重組之後達到整體形象協調的藝術手段，在菲洛諾夫的作品中充分的表現出來。前衛藝術家菲洛諾夫的創作觀念，經過一個世紀以後，似乎再現於烏克蘭哈爾科夫的藝術家羅曼·諾金的作品之中。

羅曼·諾金的作品與其他具備獨一風格的繪畫不同，採用的是綜合了各種形式的複合手法。他的作品帶有哈爾科夫設計與藝術學院的藝術特色，但更具備自己獨特的藝術造詣。哈爾科夫設計與藝術學院以及哈爾科夫地區在視覺藝術方面有著自己特殊的觀念和敏銳的超前嗅覺，羅曼身處其中，自然免不了會對新藝術形式有強烈的追求。他將室內壁畫的視野和實驗性的探索精神結合，表現在其作品的畫布之上。他最顯著的表現手段便是將顏色的種種特性盡可能發揮得淋漓盡致，交錯混亂、並置以達到幽靈般的神祕感。他的作品必須閱讀觀看全系列的作品，才能體會到其完整的風格。他利用色彩本身的特質，創作出一種新的藝術語彙。

花神之吻｜油彩·畫布
A Kiss of Flóra｜Oil on Canvas｜61x122cm｜2010

烏克蘭當代藝術家群像

事實上，羅曼這種系列性的創作手法受到現代主義的影響。二十一世紀的視覺藝術不是存在單一手段的孤立表現，而是擴展作者的主觀本質意圖。看他作品中的造型，能強烈體會到新現代主義與後現代主義的巨大影響。他偏好利用光學效果製造的輪廓，以及被描繪對象的內在的敘事，創建了一個「風格」。羅曼輕鬆地將不大相同的文化符號和聯想，透過他豐富的調色盤在畫布上進行創作，並且他的系列作品創造出不同的符號意義；在每塊畫布上，都可以看到一部真正的戲劇，矛盾衝突的藝術表現手法畫出了明亮、豐富或單純的色調，有疏有密、非常繁複又似乎零亂的畫面，使得觀眾深深感受到迷人的魅力。當然，在如此複雜多變的藝術手法背後，必然是經過深思熟慮的邏輯思考。身為善用色彩的專家，所以羅曼無法只作單一題材的表現，同時因為他也是專精的壁畫藝術家，因此他能夠輕鬆地在同一空間和平面嚴謹地安排畫面的各個部分，包括整體的節奏感和柔情的表達、畫面各個色層的相互交錯協調。

1

1. 艷陽下　Under the Sun｜油彩・畫布　Oil on Canvas｜80x100cm｜2010
2. 祈禱　Praying｜油彩・木版　Oil on Wood｜48x92cm｜1999
3. 下沈　Fall｜油彩・畫布　Oil on Canvas｜80x160cm｜1998
4. 半人馬的靈感　The Inspiration for the Centaur "The memory of the city" Series　《記憶中的城市》系列｜油彩・畫布　Oil on Canvas｜77x154cm｜2004

2

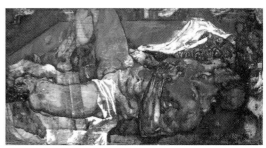

3

羅曼創作的這些特質，使得他的作品在創作的符號與想像的基礎上，製造了一個既醒目又協調的情節；這是一種綜合了各種元素的整體藝術形式。一些專家們公認他的創造性活動很有智慧和激情不是沒有原因的。因為他們看到一個組合了文化內涵、具有大型繪畫和塊狀肌理的複雜藝術形式，以及極強的藝術表現力，也可看出他在藝術設計學院所學習到專家們的專業功底。此外，這種裝飾性和感性的抒情並沒有削弱繪畫性，反而是將作品的表面特徵轉換成表達更深層次的內心狀態。

他的系列《記憶中的城市》取了一個奇特的角度，將古代雕塑和時間、空間結合在一起，同時表現在畫面上。羅曼用壁畫藝術的方式，強調了藝術的符號、建築和古文化，企圖在畫面上表現出時間流逝的痕跡。在幾何形結構組成的空間，想像出消失了的世界，幾乎所有的物件都變成抽象的片段。這樣的表現手法，也出現在1998年創作的《下沈》和1999年的《祈禱》中。這些作品的造型特殊，色彩強烈，構圖極其獨特。

4

1

2

小組畫《咖啡廳女子》系列相較於上述系列，對比較不強烈，可以被視為非具象、裝飾性和紀念性相結合的創作。宛如東方瓷器上那些明亮、清晰的色彩，以及微妙的輪廓圖形，使得這系列作品充滿音樂的旋律，不僅充滿詩意，更溢滿女性溫柔的情緒以及活力。表現主義和自由藝術的方式、寬敞的構圖被凝固在畫布上，與觀眾保持了距離，但又讓人感覺它不是一幅完全平面的作品。

近來，羅曼很明顯的傾向非具象的表現手法。新的系列《艷陽下》可以看到作家很明顯的趨向變形的表現手段。《岸邊的女子》、《撿貝殼》也可看出受到康定斯基的影響，以及較以往不同的色彩節奏。但他不能被認為是前衛藝術的簡單闡釋，畫家是在具象和抽象之間尋找接入點，並設置了女性的形象和花卉造型以及各種生物型態的元素。這個系列表現了抒情的曲調，畫面的元素都建立在柔軟的線形、建築形式和繪畫的節奏上。

3

《壓抑的熱情》和《花神之吻》喚起類似新現代主義的表現形式，具備了許多羅曼的符號特質和造型。節奏性的安排平面的輪廓，引領進入靜謐的冥想，進行深刻的沉思。雖然，解構的方法和造型的變化在這些作品並不是那麼強烈，但在美妙的《爵士樂》系列的作品則可一覽無遺。

4

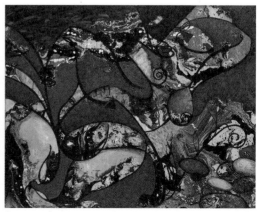

5

相較於前一個完全不同的幾何結構的詮釋，《爵士樂》系列體現了羅曼的另一個追求。畫家的繪畫設法表達生動的型態，並且結合音樂、運用當地的色彩，將物體用線條和變形手段處理。二十世紀初的藝術家，也有類似這樣子的表現手段，在畫面上釋放誘惑，引導觀者體驗在畫布上的音樂感。運用變形手段處理形象之後，爵士樂充滿了活力，且令人精神亢奮。畫面的筆觸粗獷「切割分塊面」的形式，大膽落筆準確細膩的人物精神捕捉，使畫家維持了表面的基本平衡。那些線條準確地掌控著色彩的佈局，而這種潛在的效果，在以幾何形體構成的畫作是必須的。在繪畫色彩中創造音樂感涉及到新的藝術思維，且賦予各種顏色不同的價值觀念。羅曼·諾金成功地在畫布上呈現了他的音樂。(全文完)

6

1. 咖啡廳裡的女子們　The Ladies in Café｜油彩·畫布　Oil on Canvas｜77x61cm｜2003
2. 咖啡廳裡的女子們　The Ladies in Café｜油彩·畫布　Oil on Canvas｜77x61cm｜2004
3. 壓抑的熱情　Depressed Passion｜油彩·畫布　Oil on Canvas｜70x90cm｜2010
4. 撿貝殼　Assembling a Sea Shell｜油彩·畫布　Oil on Canvas｜77x102cm｜2010
5. 岸邊的女子　Woman on a Coast of the Sea｜油彩·畫布　Oil on Canvas｜80x100cm｜2010
6. 薩克斯管演奏者　Saxophonist｜油彩·畫布　Oil on Canvas｜100x80cm｜2009

熱烈的景色襯托著三位充滿魅力的年輕女音樂家，她們演奏著當地的民間曲子，在睡蓮池塘邊，我們聽到了她們動人的音樂。

The enthusiastic view highlights the three charming and young female musicians, who play the local folk songs and we can hear their touching music next to the water lily pond.

音樂家｜油彩‧畫布
Musicians｜Oil on Canvas｜77x102cm｜2011

巧妙安排條狀的紫色，河水的藍色與橙色的沙灘和樹形成鮮明而強烈的對比。一片熱鬧的氣氛，好像聽到了水中美女嬉戲的喧嘩聲。岸上兩位女孩正在蠢蠢欲動，她們馬上要加入河裡的遊戲。

The deliberately arranged purple strips, the blue river, the orange beach, form a strong contrast with trees. In a bustling atmosphere, we seem to hear the noises of the beauties playing in the water. The two girls on the shore cannot wait to join them in the water.

河邊戲水｜油彩・畫布
Swim in the Stream｜Oil on Canvas｜80x80cm｜2011

(左圖)公主的散步-I｜油彩・畫布
(Left) Walking Princess-I｜Oil on Canvas｜120x40cm｜2011

(右上圖)女人會議｜油彩・畫布
(Upper Right) Intrigue ｜Oil on Canvas｜61x92cm｜2011

(右下圖)夜晚的露台｜油彩・畫布
(Lower Right) Night Terrace ｜Oil on Canvas｜51x92cm｜2011

《公主散步》裡，童話裡的公主牽著綠色的怪獸寵物悠閒地散步，傲慢又自得。平面處理的繪畫肌理以及畫面結構的黑、白、灰的處理和安排，冷暖色彩的巧妙對比更加突顯出主體的性格。畫面華麗而輕鬆。

In "Walking Princess", the princess in a fairy tale is walking her green pet monster with casualty, seeming arrogant and carefree. The painting context with plane processing and the color-block arrangement of black, grey and white colors, while the deliberately contrast of cold and warm colors are highlight the characteristics of the body more, giving a glamorous and easy perception to the painting.

在秋天的日子裡，年輕的媽媽推著嬰兒車在落英紛飛的天空下散步，她輕輕地搖動著推車，彷彿在唱著「乖乖睡，我的寶貝……」。

In autumn days, a young mother pushes the stroller to stroll under the cherry blossom. She gently pushes the stroller and sings the lullaby.

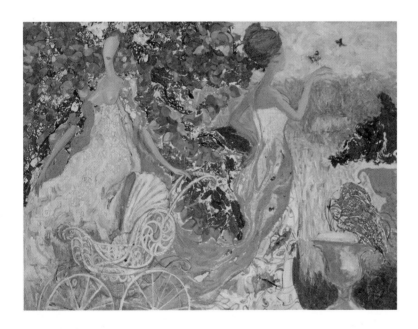

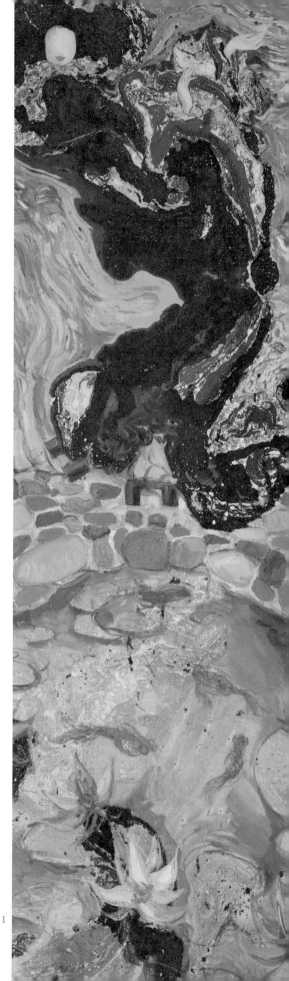

(左上圖)風和日麗｜油彩‧畫布
(Upper Left) Serenity ｜ Oil on Canvas｜77x102cm｜ 2011

(左下圖)搖籃曲｜油彩‧畫布
(Lower Left) Lullaby ｜ Oil on Canvas｜70x90cm｜ 2012

(右圖)跳舞的金魚｜油彩‧畫布
(Right) Dancing Goldfish ｜Oil on Canvas｜120x40cm｜ 2011

(上圖)溫暖的海洋-Ⅰ|油彩‧畫布
(Upper) Warm Ocean - Ⅰ |Oil on Canvas|80x100cm| 2011

(中圖)溫暖的海洋-Ⅱ|油彩‧畫布
(Middle) Warm Ocean - Ⅱ |Oil on Canvas|80x100cm| 2011

(下圖)溫暖的海洋-Ⅲ|油彩‧畫布
(Lower) Warm Ocean - Ⅲ |Oil on Canvas|80x100cm| 2011

我喜歡將我的感受以象徵性圖像表達出來,進而描繪出人類或物體的內在本質。

在這些象徵性的圖像裡,隱藏了更深一層的含意。

我希望觀眾在欣賞我的作品時,能夠從這些本質裡感受到我內在的情緒。

- 羅曼自述 -

滲透│油彩·畫布

Interpenetration │ Oil on Canvas │ 61x92cm │ 2011

活潑明亮的顏色，熱情的芭蕾舞蹈，使人想起韓德爾的《水上音樂》。

The bright colors and passionate ballet remind us of the Water Music by Handel.

水上舞蹈-I｜油彩·畫布
Dancing on the Water -I｜Oil on Canvas｜77x102cm｜2011

(上圖)木蘭花下的午後｜油彩·畫布
(Upper) Evening Under the Magnolia｜Oil on Canvas｜51x92cm｜2011

(下圖)公園裡的煙火｜油彩·畫布
(Lower) Fireworks in the Park｜Oil on Canvas｜51x92cm｜2011

《魅力》裡，照鏡的黑美人呈S形，縱向切割畫幅，主宰了紫、鈷藍、綠色與橘黃、玫瑰紅的
對比。這是一幅熱情洋溢的傑作。

In "Enchantment", the black beauty in the reflection of the mirror is in an S-shape style,
vertically dividing the painting into two parts and dominating the contrast of purple, dark
blue, green, orange-yellow, and rose-red colors. This is a masterpiece of passion.

(左圖)樹蔭｜油彩‧畫布
(Left) In the Shadow of a Large Tree ｜ Oil on Canvas ｜ 61x92cm ｜ 2012

(右圖)魅力｜油彩‧畫布
(Right) Enchantment ｜ Oil on Canvas ｜ 70x90cm ｜ 2011

烏克蘭當代藝術家群像

《記憶中的城市》系列作品結合各種具代表性元素的符號，如：藝術、建築、自然、科學發明等等，展現了在不同的時代，人類對精神文明的努力探索和執著的追求，並且表達了在追求探索過程之中所產生的美感。這些元素也典型的代表了人類文明發展進程中的各個時代的精神象徵，以及歷史變遷所留下的刻痕。

作者運用簡約的色彩描述主體，並且利用複雜的多層次的肌理製作背景，有機地將一些貌似不相干又各具不同邏輯的思維方式所產生的形象巧妙地容納在同一個畫面裡，使作品產生出意想不到的諧和的現代特色。

畫作雖然屬於較具象的創作風格，但其本質卻是抽象的精神，則既有深沈的懷舊情懷，又有凝聚時空轉換瞬變過程的幻念，主題既嚴肅但又帶有歐洲人特具的詼諧趣味。作者塑造了一種獨特的觀察視野，使得觀者在欣賞作品藝術性的同時，還能夠對歷史的演變產生深刻的思考和濃厚的興趣。畫幅雖然不大，但包羅的內涵十分豐富，屬於具備歷史長卷敘述方式的壁畫風格。

In the series of "The Memory of the City", the work combines various signs or representative elements, including art, architecture, nature and science, which exhibit the human efforts in exploration and persistence in pursuit of spiritual culture in different times, in addition to expressing the aesthetics resulted from the pursuit of exploration. These elements also represent the spiritual symbol of different times during the development process of human civilization and the traces left behind by changes of history.

The artist applies minimal colors to describe the body, using complex and multi-layered context to be the background, so that images resulted from seemingly irrelevance but with thinking of different logics, are deliberately put into one image. The work produces a surprisingly harmonious modern characteristic.

The nature of the painting contains abstract spirit despite of its more concrete creative style. It contains a profoundly nostalgia with the fantasy of instantaneous changes in the cohesion of the time and spatial conversion. The theme is both serious and comes with the specific wit and humor of Europeans. The artist has built an exceptional observing horizon so that the viewers can grow profound thoughts and strong interests for the evolution of history while appreciating the artistic quality of the works. Despite of the painting size, the content comprised is highly abundant and attributed to a mural style of historical scroll description.

失敗的愛情宣言 －《記憶中的城市》系列｜油彩‧畫布
The Failure Declaration of Love - "The Memory of the City" series｜70x140cm｜2011

揚帆的航船在大海中急駛，隨著洶湧的波濤起伏。海鷗在船邊飛翔，意味著海灣就在附近了。看哪，海邊露台上，身著長裙的貴婦正在竊竊私語，假面舞會正在進行。

The sailing boat is hurtling on the ocean and follows the stormy waters to go up and down. The seagull flies by the boat, implying the bay is nearby. Look at the platform by the sea, the noble women dressed in long skirts are murmuring while the masquerade ball is going on.

(左圖)遙望航船 | 油彩・畫布
(Left) Looking at the Fleet of Sailing | Oil on Canvas | 80x100cm | 2012

(右上圖)瀑布旋律 | 油彩・畫布
(Upper Right) Melody of the Waterfall | Oil on Canvas | 61x92cm | 2012

(右下圖)散步瀑布旁 | 油彩・畫布
(Lower Right) Walk by the Waterfall | Oil on Canvas | 70x90cm | 2012

琴聲如瀑布般流淌，流入人們的心中。美，盡在不言中。

The sound of violin is flowing like a waterfall into people's minds. There are no words that can be used to describe this kind of beauty.

秋日，少婦推著嬰兒車踏著滿地落葉，秋風拂面而來，優雅，清閒。

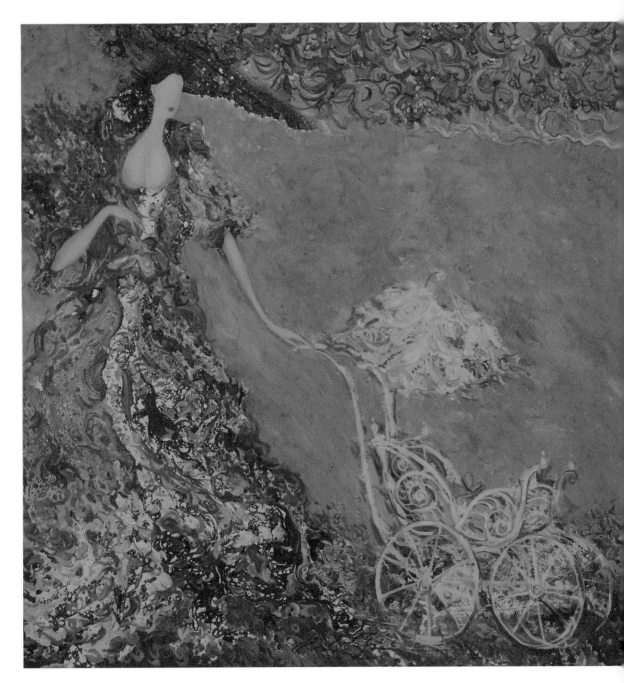

步行｜油彩·畫布

Walk｜Oil on Canvas｜80x80cm｜2012

姐妹們在繁花盛開的季節翩翩起舞。寶石般繽紛的藤葉和隨風飄落的花瓣,融進了如花的女孩。

The girls are dancing in a blooming season whereas the jewel-like vine leaves and pedals floating with the wind is blended with the girls.

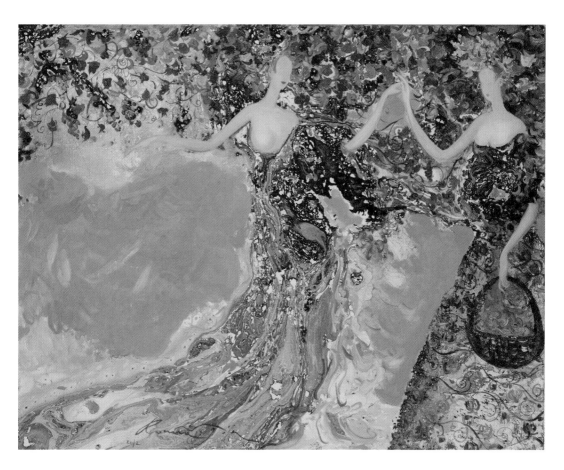

姐妹 | 油彩・畫布
Sisters | Oil on Canvas | 70x90cm | 2012

灰紫色的裸體在寶石藍的海水中沐浴，濺起了層層浪花。人物傾斜的造型使得畫面呈現強烈的動感。海水的嘩嘩聲和女孩的嬉笑聲，組成了美妙的大海交響曲。

The gray-purple nudity is bathing in the sapphire ocean, splashing layers of waves. The tilted figures present a strong movement to the image. The rushing sound of the ocean and the laughter of the girls together compose a wonderful symphony of the ocean.

沐浴｜油彩·畫布
Bathing｜Oil on Canvas｜70x90cm｜2012

三位女神在蓮花池裡翩翩起舞，旋轉的舞姿令人眼花繚亂。這是一首約翰·史特勞斯的圓舞曲。

The three goddesses dance on the lotus pool, whose rotating dance bedazzles everyone. This is a Waltz composed by John Strauss.

水上舞蹈-II｜油彩·畫布
Dancing on the Water - II｜Oil on Canvas｜77x102cm｜2012

2011年的《島嶼》開啓了另一個世界。這個系列雖然能看到一絲前期作品的影子，因為都是在歌唱，但卻從熱情的爵士樂變幻為優雅的詠嘆曲調。《島嶼》中，美麗的大海女神托起了航船，海藻和繁花點綴的長髮隨著季風飄拂。小島的燈塔和建築物隱藏其中，這是克里米亞的島嶼，一個熱情的島嶼，一個充滿著人情味和希望的島嶼。

The 2011 "Island" has opened up another world. Although we can observe the impact from the previous works, the singing has turned the passionate jazz music into elegant chant melody. In "Island", the beautiful goddess of the ocean has lifted up the sailing boat, whereas the long hair decorated with seaweed and flowers are carried by the monsoon. The island towers and buildings are hidden within. This is one passionate Crimea island that is filled with friendship and hope.

島嶼｜油彩‧畫布
Island｜Oil on Canvas｜92x122cm｜2011

善於運用色彩的羅曼於2012年的新作《殖民地夢想系列》中，除了延續以往對女性美的禮讚之外，他採用象徵主義手法結合當代繪畫觀念，創作了一批象徵性的女神畫像，將我們的傳統視覺習慣變幻成更為開闊的想像空間和視野。

大海中的島嶼有著許多神秘而動人的傳說，她們孕育了一代又一代的生靈。羅曼將她們描繪成有著濃密髮辮的女神，優雅的沐著習習海風，浮游於茫茫大海之上，她們是一座座流動的島嶼。

畫作中，我們可以感受到畫家對古今探險家的禮讚；因為從古到今，許多航海家為著發現和探索新的生存空間獻出了畢生精力，他們駕馭帆船歷經千難萬險發現了一個個的島嶼，譜寫了一段段生動感人的驚險篇章。

在篇章中，畫家同時捕捉了時間流逝、空間變幻過程中的寶貴瞬刻，創造了奇妙的童話般的意境以及穿越時空的想像力。甜美的人物造型和高雅的灰色對比系列色彩的應用，使得畫作成為了一篇篇抒情的散文詩。觀者被引入一座虛幻的美麗花園，在這裡，只有輕柔如搖籃曲般的歌聲，和那令人尊敬的大地之母……

Eastern European artist Roman Nogin good at using colors has recently completed some new works. In "Colonial Dream" series of 2012, Other than his extension of praise for female aesthetics, he applies approaches of symbolism combined with modern painting concepts to create a group of symbolic portraits of the goddess. He turns the traditional visual habits into fantasy of broader imaginary space and horizon.

The islands in the ocean come with various mysterious and touching legends, which have incubated generations of beings. Roman portrayed them as the goddess with thick and dense braids who were gracefully took the sea breeze and floated on the ocean. They were the floating islands.

We perceive the painter's praise for ancient and modern explorers from the painting due to navigators' lifelong efforts dedicated to the discovery and exploration of new space for survival from the past to now. They maneuvered the sailing boat and underwent hardship to only discover many different islands and composed various vivid, touching and adventurous chapters.

The painter captures the valuable moment of time passing and spatial changes from the chapters, creates a wonderful artistic conception of fairy tales and the imagination that travels through time and space. The sweet characters form contrast with the elegant gray color, and the application of series colors, have turned the painting into lyrical prose poem, introducing us to a virtual and beautiful garden. Only gentle songs like the lullabies are found with the respectful Mother Earth.

探險，探險，海上的探險家們都十分鐘情於發現新的
島嶼。你看，無風的海面上航行著中國和歐洲的帆
船，海上出現了幻影般美麗的島嶼女神，她的長髮編
成了萬能的阿拉丁神燈。這是所有航海者的夢想，作
者為我們描繪出一幅神奇似夢幻般的童話世界。

Adventure, adventure! The ocean explorers are
all passionate about discovering the new islands.
Look at the Chinese and European failing boats
on the windless sea. When the island goddess with
mirage beauty appears on the ocean, her long hair
is braided into the magical lamp of Aladdin. This is
the dream of all sailors. The author depicts a magic
and fantastic fairy tale world for the viewers.

島嶼《殖民地夢想系列》｜油彩·畫布
Island "Colonial Dream" series｜Oil on Canvas｜90x145cm｜2012

如童話般的夢，遠征的帆船隊航行在美麗的群島之間，島嶼似美人，隱藏著鳥群的茂密植被就是她們的髮飾，散發著芳香，吸引著探險家們的感官。一座座流動的島嶼是大地之母，她們吟唱著古老的歌謠。輕柔海風中，飄來一曲曲美妙的大海之歌。

Such fairy like dream whereas expediting sailing team is sailing between the beautiful islands. The islands resemble the beauties, whereas the flocks of birds hidden act as their hair accessories that emit fragrance to attract the senses of the explorers. The floating islands are the Mother Earth who chants the ancient lullaby. The wonderful songs of ocean are accompanied by the gentle breeze.

群島《殖民地夢想系列》｜油彩・畫布
Archipelago "Colonial Dream" series｜Oil on Canvas｜90x145cm｜2012

《秋裝》是一個生命的過程，秋葉綻放美麗的過程。秋之女神將她的葉子飄然撒下，回歸大地。樹葉由翠綠變成枯黃是一種生命的輪迴。秋天的落葉是為了迎接嚴寒的冬天，以及接踵而來芬芳的春天和絢麗的夏天。這，不是終結，而是新的開始。樹葉雖然隕落但她的靈魂卻獲得了重生—— 新芽正在悄悄地萌動。大自然賦予萬物以生命，宛如女神頭頂髮辮般的植被呵護著人類，亞當和夏娃得以孕育新的生命，延續了希望。象徵幻想的落花掉進了童話中女孩的狗兒拖車裡。

"Dress Autumn" is a process of life and a processof autumn leaves radiating their beauty. The goddess of autumn drops her leaves and return to the mother earth. The tree leaves turning from green to yellow is a cycle of life. The falling leaves of autumn aims to greet the harsh winter, the following fragrant spring and the brilliant summer. This is not the end but a new beginning. Although the leaves fall, her soul get rebirth, as the sprouts are quietly germinating. The nature bestows life to all beings similar to the goddess carrying braided-hair like vegetation that pamper the human, so that Adam and Even can cultivate new life and extend the hope. The falling flowers symbolizing fantasy falls into the dog trailer of the girl in a fairy tale.

(左圖)公主散步—II｜油彩・畫布
(Left) Walking Princess - II｜Oil on Canvas｜90x130cm｜2012

(右圖)秋裝｜油彩・畫布
(Right) Dress Autumn｜Oil on Canvas｜90x145cm｜2012

CHAPTER 4.

滄茫的歷程。

－娜塔莎　*Natasha Perekhodenko*

自古以來，有許多描繪時光永恆的藝術作品出現過，而烏克蘭年輕的女畫家娜塔莎創作的油畫《漫長的歷程》卻給我們帶來一種全新的夢幻般的感覺，清新、純淨而透明。畫面中有恆古的山崖、荒漠、大海、島嶼、天空和浮雲。水中浮雲的倒影顯得整個畫面十分靜謐，似乎在無言地訴說著流傳了千萬年的古老童話故事。山崖的頂尖呈螺旋狀，像是兩隻海螺化石，當海風吹過，它們會發出嗚嗚的樂聲，為美妙的童話伴奏。它們的出現，也恰好表現作者企圖表達的宇宙間滄海桑田變化無窮的漫長歷程主題。

在同系列作品《靈魂山谷》、《爬行》和《恆山》中，娜塔莎同樣運用了眾所周知的隱喻，蝸牛和烏龜都是行動緩慢的動物，但也是古老而長壽的生物。它們的出現，意味著歷史進程的悠遠和亙古。

作者在畫布上多次打磨顏料層，使得油畫具有磨漆畫的豐富肌理和層次。局部如小島部分，用筆桿刻畫出自然裂紋肌理，又有版畫的效果。畫面保留的稀薄流淌的松節油斑跡，使灰白色的山體，更有著如大理石的高貴的斑痕。

娜塔莎的構圖很巧妙，變形的兩個錐形三角打破了水平線和天空的均衡感，加之精心安排看似隨意塗撒的深色零碎肌理，使得畫面具有一種不安定的運動感覺，結合天空上的渦狀線條，神奇地演變出超越二度空間的音樂感。水中的那根白色線條連接了錐狀的山體和水中的橢圓，如同樂隊的指揮棒一樣，成為穩定畫面構成的要素，這是典型當代繪畫理性抽象的手法。

她採用象徵抒情的手法來抒發自己的感受，看得出來她具有很純熟的繪畫技巧，其造型既帶裝飾風格但又有強烈的繪畫感，平面又不失厚實，單純又含複雜的變化。主題看似直接但內涵極深，屬於其特有的歐洲純真的人文特色，耐人尋味，真誠地呈現出她心中的克里米亞半島寶石般的璀璨陽光，大海和山石，為觀眾唱出了一首委婉動人的童話詩歌。

漫長的歷程｜油彩・畫布
Long Voyage｜Oil on Canvas｜77x102cm｜2011

靈魂山谷｜油彩・畫布
Valley of the Spirits｜Oil on Canvas｜75x110cm｜2011

Since ancient times, many artworks are created to describe the eternity of time, however the young female painter from Ukraine, Natasha, created this oil painting "Long Voyage", which brings us a brand new dreamy feeling, it is fresh, pure, and transparent. There are the ancient mountains, the isolated desert, the ocean, the islands, the sky and the floating clouds in the picture. The reflection of the floating clouds in the water makes the whole picture very peaceful. Seemingly it is telling wordlessly an ancient fairy tale that has been around for tens of millions of years. The top of the mountain is shaped as spirals, which looks like two conch fossils. When the sea breezes through, they make the "ooooh" sounds and become the accompaniment music of the wonderful fairy tales. Their appearance, happen to point out the painter's attempt to describe the theme, which is the endless variation of the long history around the universe

In "Valley of the Spirits", "Climbing" and "The Ancient Mountains", the works of a same series, Natasha used the well-known metaphor of snails and turtles for they are both slow-moving animals and at the same time are ancient and longevous creatures. Their appearance means the endless and everlasting historical process.

The painter polishes the colors on the canvas again and again, to make the oil painting full of rich texture and layers like a grinding painting. In parts, like the part of the island, she uses the shaft of the pen to make it more like a natural cracks texture, as well as the effect of a woodblock painting. The flowing trace of the turpentine oil on the picture makes the texture on the off-white mountains nobler like marbles.

Natasha's sketching is masterstroke. The two deformed triangular cones break the balance between the horizon and the sky. The carefully arranged dark-colored fragmented texture looks as if it is casually painted, which makes the picture looks unstable as if there is movement there. Furthermore, it connects with the whirlpool lines in the sky, which marvelously evolved into the music that is above two dimensions. The white line in the water connects with the cone-shaped mountain and the ovals in the water, it is as if a music conductor waves his baton and stabilized the whole picture. This is classic technique of modern painting, rational abstraction.

She uses the method that symbolizes sentiment to express her own feelings. It can be found from here that her painting techniques are very skillful, its shape is not only in decorating style but also features a very strong sense of painting. It is planar, however does not lose its thickness. It is simple, however contains complicated variations. The theme looks as if it is straight and simple, however in fact deep. It shows the painter's pure unique European cultural characteristics, which is very interesting. Moreover, it also represents the bright sunshine, the ocean and the mountains of Crimea Peninsula in her heart, it is as if it's singing a beautiful poetic fairy song for the audience.

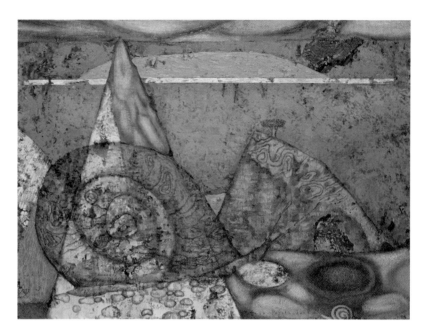

爬行｜油彩·畫布
Climbing｜Oil on Canvas｜77x102cm｜2011

恆山｜油彩·畫布
The Ancient Mountains｜Oil on Canvas｜77x102cm｜2011

克里米亞半島(Crimea Peninsula)位於歐洲的南部，黑海北部海岸上的一個半島，目前是烏克蘭的一個自治共和國。這裡的氣候屬地中海氣候，溫暖潮溼，且風景壯麗優美，是著名的旅遊療養聖地，也是少數能夠看到烏克蘭文化古蹟的地區。在果園、葡萄園和樹木的掩映下，散落著許多村莊、清真寺、修道院，以及俄羅斯皇家宮殿以及古希臘和中世紀的城堡。

這個地方對烏克蘭的藝術家來說，是靈感來源的聖地。多數的藝術家都會到這裡寫生、創作，娜塔莎也不例外。我們從她的作品中，可以看到這裡天空的色彩、文化遺跡的生命力，以及靜謐美好的次元空間。

克里米亞 | 油彩·畫布
Demerji | Oil on Canvas | 114x166cm | 1999

娜塔莎對於非洲和南美洲的民族文化非常感興趣；非洲面具和馬雅的精神系列，將作者腦海裡對於當地的文化遺產和風格的印象深刻表現出來。生動活潑且富有情感的來緩和線性的節奏感，可塑性的風格化、程式化，輪廓和色彩、空間的發揮，都賦予這些作品非常逼真的表現力。

馬雅精神-II｜油彩‧畫布
Spirits of Maya - II｜Oil on Canvas｜100x100cm｜2005

Natasha is very interested in the folk culture in Africa and South America. The African masks and the Maya Spirit series depict the artist's deep impression of the cultural heritages and styles. These works are given efforts of realistic performance through the lively, vivid and emotional source with linear rhythm, stylized scalability, programming and contour, and the elaboration of colors and space.

馬雅精神-I | 油彩・畫布
Spirits of Maya - I | Oil on Canvas | 100x100cm | 2005

看得出來，娜塔莎很愛看書，也愛思索。她的畫很單純：寧靜的街景、茂盛的植物，日常的靜物以至呈幾何形體的山石、蝸牛、烏龜等等都是她入畫的對象。她的畫似乎都帶有裝飾風格，可是你多看一下，就會發現娜塔莎在用畫帶領著觀眾思考：當人類一代又一代生之滅之的同時，歷經千百萬年的大自然卻似乎恆久地存在，它留給人們最好的禮物永遠是安詳、靜謐、平和的印象。

在當今紛亂的世界中，人類的心中卻永遠為這個美好的印象留有一席空間。當我們痛苦的時候，它會成為慰藉的良藥。娜塔莎用她的心靈在感動著人們。

她的畫面雖然簡潔但經過精心佈局，幾何形體的穿插排列、多種色彩肌理的佈局、黑白灰色塊大小對比的相互呼應、反透視的現代造型手段等等，都被她精巧而不露聲色地運用在畫作裡面，而她的原則就是樸實和真誠！

It is clear to see that Natasha loves reading and thinking. Her paintings are simple, quite street views, lush plants, daily static objects, and any mountain rocks, snails, turtle, and any object with geometric shape can become the objects of her painting. Her paintings seem to be all in a decorative style. However, upon a close look, you will discover that Natasha is leading the viewers to think through her painting. While humans distinguished generation by generation, the Nature undergone hundreds of thousands years seems to exist in eternity, which also leaves people with the best gifts of eternal serenity, tranquility and peace.

In chaotic world today, people are preserving a space for this beautiful impression in mind. It becomes a consolation medicine, whereas Natasha moves people with her soul.

Her paintings are simplistic yet deliberately arranged, whereas including the interspersed arrangement of geometric shapes, layout of multiple colors and contexts, mutual correspondence of contrasts in black, white and gray blocks as well as size comparison, and the modern modeling means of anti-perspectives, are all implemented in her paintings meticulously without showing emotions. Her principles are based on humbleness and sincerity.

我喜歡裝飾主義的表現手法。我試著表達我的心情、感受和想法,
　　　不只是利用物品現實描繪的手法,而是使用這些物品的形象。
　我喜歡將現實誇大,簡化形式,並且用我自己的方法賦予物品更多生命力。
　我嘗試創作樂觀積極的畫作,希望觀眾們能夠用輕鬆的態度去欣賞我的作品。

- 娜塔莎自述 -

作者以嫻熟的手法，採用裝飾誇張的風格描繪了兩棵生機盎然的大樹。紅雲在畫中扮演點睛的作用，地上一團白色的水窪，與其呼應。這幅作品可以看到作者應該是受到澳洲和非洲岩壁畫的啟示。

The artist applies skillful techniques to depict two vital trees using decorative and exaggerating styles. The red cloud highlights the painting with correspondence to the white puddle on the ground. This painting shows the artist's inspiration from the Australian and African murals.

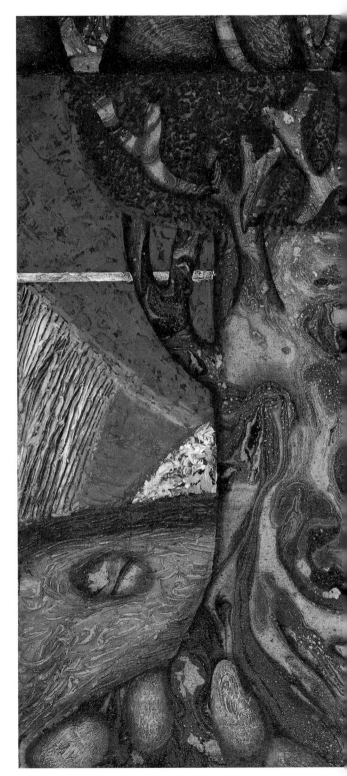

樹｜油彩‧畫布
Trees｜Oil on Canvas｜77x102cm｜2010

白貓來訪｜油彩・畫布
The White Cat Came to Visit｜Oil on Canvas｜61x92cm｜2010

克里米亞半島，山上，童話般的石屋，石階通向大海。娜娜的小樹隨海風輕輕搖曳。濃濃的雲層籠罩著大海，白帆點點……

小屋的門邊，貓兒在向遠處眺望，盼望主人歸來。娜塔莎使用了稍微變形的手法，描繪了一個寧靜的時刻。

In the Crimea Peninsula , the fairy-like stone house built on the mountain with stairway towards the ocean. The small trees are swinging with the sea breeze and the thick clouds covering the ocean.

Natasha has applied a slightly deformed method, including the white sails and cat overlooking by the cabin door for the return of its owner to depict a tranquil moment.

溫馨的主題：海灣一角，石屋窗台上的瓶花和果盤。熱烈的暗紅色，橘黃的海灘與深藍的海水形成對比。這是一幅美妙的熱帶海灣抒情爵士樂。

Cozy Theme: A corner of a bay, where the vase and fruit tray by the windowsill. The passionate dark red and the orange-yellow beach form contrast with the dark-blue Ocean. This is a wonderfully lyrical jazz music of tropical bay.

窗戶旁｜油彩·畫布
On the Window｜Oil on Canvas｜51x61cm｜2006

娜塔莎的靜物畫透露出她心中炙熱的情感，李子、切開的梨、瓶花、高腳酒杯、茶壺、窺視籠中小鳥的貓咪，以及窗外的景色等等，無一不是表達了她對生活情節的深愛與關注。她以極大的熱情和興趣，巧妙地運用色彩構成和幾何造型等現代表現手法。同時，她熱情地關懷著身邊的物件，娓娓敘述著幸福生活的種種細節。變形誇張更有個性的圖像，強烈刺激著觀眾的目光，使其作品具備深刻的感染力度。

綠茶｜油彩·畫布
Green Tea｜Oil on Canvas｜60x60cm｜2008

(上圖)私人興趣-I｜油彩・畫布
(Upper) Personal Interest -I｜Oil on Canvas｜50x100cm｜2005

(下圖)私人興趣-II｜油彩・畫布
(Lower) Personal Interest -II｜Oil on Canvas｜50x100cm｜2005

The still life paintings of Natasha revealed the vigor of her emotions —prunes, cut pears, vase of flowers, goblets, teapots, the cat peering at the caged bird, and the scenery outside of the window... are all the symbols of her love and care of life. With a great passion and enthusiasm, she cleverly used the color composition and geometric modeling and other modern expression techniques. At the same time, she cared about surrounding objects with passion, and tirelessly described all the details about her blessed life. Exaggerated, deformed, and characteristic images and the profound intensity of her works strongly attract the viewers' attention.

花束｜油彩‧畫布
Bouquet | Oil on Canvas | 77x102cm | 2005

(上圖)變形｜油彩‧畫布
(Upper) Metamorphoses｜Oil on Canvas｜77x102cm｜2007

(下圖)鬱悶白日｜油彩‧畫布
(Lower) Lemon Midday｜Oil on Canvas｜77x102cm｜2007

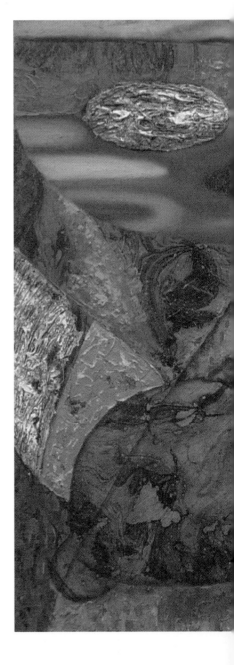

(上圖)窗外｜油彩‧畫布
(Upper) Outside the Window｜Oil on Canvas｜50x50cm｜2002

(下圖)黃色窗台｜油彩‧畫布
(Lower) Yellow Sill｜Oil on Canvas｜60x50cm｜2002

(右圖)雨后｜油彩‧畫布
(Right) After Rain｜Oil on Canvas｜77x110cm｜2006

雨後的山脈清新醒目，浮雲翩翩，繞山而過。日日復日日，年年復年年，歷經多少滄桑，山還是那麼巍峨。大自然的造物神奇又親切。畫中運用了許多不同質感的肌理，使得簡明的主題變得似夢幻般的深邃。

CHAPTER 5.

抒情的詩境。

—亞歷克山大 *Alexander Serdyuk*

亞歷克山大創作出了一系列優雅的抒情詩般的畫作。在其作品中，我們可以感受到他對生活，對大自然無限眷戀和熱愛的樸實情愫，並且深深地為之所感動。他用薄霧般美妙的紗縵，輕柔地覆蓋在作為詩歌中的音符如：現實中的人物、景物和靜物之上。畫中靜謐的景象緩緩地在一個神秘的空間中運行，瞬息萬變的時光得以延伸和開拓⋯⋯

《夢》中有個睡著的年輕女孩，她正做什麼夢呢？透過畫家的筆，我們可以清楚感受到女孩的夢肯定是愉快的；剛剛從野外採摘來的白色鮮花插滿了玻璃瓶，女孩捏著其中的一支，愜意地趴在皺摺如絲絨般的藍色背襯前睡著了。畫家為我們展現了一個美好的、詩意的花的夢境。

Alexander has created a series of elegant and lyrical paintings, in which we could see and be touched by his simple sincerity of nostalgia and love to the nature. He gently covered the poetic melody such as real characters, landscape and still life with misty amazing silks. The tranquil scenes slowly move in a mysterious space, extending and opening up the changing times...

"Dreams" depicts a sleeping young girl. What is she dreaming of ? We can clearly perceive the pleasure of the girl's dream through the brush of the painter. The white flowers just picked up from the field are arranged into the glass vase, whereas the girl is holding one of the flowers, casually lying on the wrinkled and yet velvety blue shirt and falling asleep. The painter has exhibited a beautiful and poetic dream of flowers.

(右圖)夢｜油彩·畫布
(Right) Dreams｜Oil on Canvas｜102x76cm｜2010

透過主觀安排處理後的靜物組合，體現了畫家對藝術創作純真的熱愛和強烈的感受。大面積的暗綠色背景、代表了畫家精神的畫架、調色板，和帶民族風情有紅蝴蝶結的小帽，形成強烈的對比，更加突出了主題。憑藉主觀感覺來安排環境和物件，而非機械性的複製描繪對象的實際形體，以達到自然的有機結合。畫家將自己的情感和生活態度轉移到畫布上，將靜物換化為其情感的代言人，活生生的訴說其精神感受。

Through the arrangement of subjectively processed still life combinations, the painter has expressed the strong feelings and pure passion to art creations. A large area of dark green background, the easel and palette that represent the artist's spirit and the hat decorated with ethnic red ribbon; the sharp contrast emphasized the theme much more. The organic integration of the nature was achieved by the arrangement of the environment and objects by subjective feelings instead of mechanical replication of the actual shape of the objects. The painter transferred his own feelings and living attitude on to the canvas, changing the still life to the spokesperson of his emotions who lively reveals his spiritual feelings.

(左圖)休假日│油彩・畫布
(Left) Non Working Days│Oil on Canvas│102x76cm│2011

我們可看出，在《梨子靜物》畫中，造型的設計和視覺圖像的思想意圖得以充分的結合，創造了一個全新的表達符號，拉大了與傳統造型藝術表現的距離。尤其是作品中的圖像，將畫家的創作概念和傳統藝術表現的分界點徹底表達出來。作品除了具有明顯的後現代表現手法之外，從對色調的掌控和配置安排的效果中，我們能欣賞到非常完整的構圖以及和諧的表達手段。輪廓式的物件宛如象形文字般的隱喻，鮮明地強調出作品的節奏感。

(左圖)梨子靜物｜油彩•畫布
(Left) Still Life with Pears｜Oil on Canvas｜76x102cm｜2011

(右圖)假期｜油彩•畫布
(Right) Holiday｜Oil on Canvas｜102x76cm｜2011

(上圖)梨子｜油彩‧畫布
(Upper) Pears｜Oil on Canvas｜40x55cm｜2012

(下圖)瓶子靜物｜油彩‧畫布
(Lower) Still Life with Bottles｜Oil on Canvas｜40x55cm｜2012

(右圖)等待｜油彩‧畫布
(Right) Waiting for｜Oil on Canvas｜102x76cm｜2011

忐忑不安的少女，正在等待……也許是心愛的人即將來訪，鮮藍綠的色調帶出少女那顆不安卻雀躍的心。

The uneasy girl is waiting...perhaps it is her loved one coming to visit. The blue and green color tone has highlighted the uneasy and yet winged heart of the girl.

Два Александра
СЕРДЮКА
Харьков

живопись   скульптура

(左圖)花束｜油彩‧畫布
(Left) Bouquet｜Oil on Canvas｜76x102cm｜2012

(右圖)野花｜油彩‧畫布
(Right) Wildflowers｜Oil on Canvas｜70x50cm｜2012

女孩與貓｜油彩・畫布
The Lady with Cat｜Oil on Canvas｜90x60cm｜2011

作家的創作受13-14世紀文藝復興時期的藝術大師影響極大,那時的簡約構圖和壁畫技巧深深吸引著他。他嘗試以極簡主義的方式來表達情緒,不被現實的模特兒或照片所影響,用主觀重構的人物來組成作品, 力求達到極其純粹的主觀境界。沈睡的裸體人物,既簡約又不失厚重,同端坐回眸的小貓形成靜中有動的對比,增加了作品生動的活力。從構圖上來講,人物形成畫面的對角線,與呈點狀的小貓有機的統一在畫面上,既均衡又不失衝突,是中世紀壁畫構圖風格的再現。

The artist's creations were greatly influenced by the Renaissance masters in 13-14 centuries, the minimalist composition and mural techniques has deeply attracted to him. He tried to express the emotions with minimalist methods, and not being limited by real models or photos, he strived to achieve the extreme pure subjective realm with the works composed with subjective reconstructed characters. The simple yet heavy sleeping nude figures formed a quiet-to-lively contrast with the sitting kitten that looks back, and increased the vivid vitality to the work. On the composition aspect, the figure forming the diagonal line of the picture is organically united on the scene with spottily painted kitten, the whole balanced yet conflict scene is truly the reproduce of medieval frescoes composition style.

（左圖）水罐｜油彩・畫布
(Left) Jugs｜Oil on Canvas｜55x70cm｜2012

（右圖）好多想法｜油彩・畫布
(Right) Various Thoughts｜Oil on Canvas｜100x80cm｜2012

亞歷克山大作品的特色是：大面積的平鋪又時時出現局部的肌理表現，使作品既平凡親切但又有精彩的部分再現，所以非常的耐看。大量運用強烈對比的手段來突出主體。黑白關係和色彩關係處理也是同樣的運用大面積的處理手法，讓觀者懷著輕鬆的心情來欣賞作品的同時又能深深感受到作者的情懷。

The characteristics of Alexander's works include the follows: Large area of plain with partial texture performance to give the works with ordinary, friendly and spectacular partial reproduction that is quite engaging. He uses large amount of strong contrast means to highlight the body while the black and white relation, and the color relations, are applied with large-area processing. The viewers can appreciate the work through relaxation while profoundly perceive the feelings of the artist.

蘆葦｜油彩·畫布
Reed｜Oil on Canvas｜60x80cm｜2012

對我而言，藝術是畫家自我感覺的表達。
我不是機械的複製描繪對象的實際形體，
我是憑藉主觀感覺來安排環境和物件，
以達到自然的有機結合。
我將自己的情感和生活態度轉移到畫布上，
那些靜物就是我情感的代言人。
他們活生生的代替我訴說我的精神感受。

- 亞歷克山大自述 -

農婦悠閒的步行於村莊裡，這是一個烏克蘭典型的淳樸農莊。畫家刻意以非常淡雅的紅色營造出一股特殊的氣氛，難以言狀的寧靜而祥和的空間。

The countrywoman casually walks in the village. This is a typical rustic farming village in Ukraine. The painter deliberately creates a special atmosphere using a highly elegant, light-red color to depict an unspeakable tranquility and a harmonious space.

村莊裡｜油彩·畫布
In the Village｜Oil on Canvas｜50x70cm｜2012

烏克蘭鄉間，黃昏時候悠哉散步的婦人和孩子，在大自然的陪伴下，十分安寧和滿足。遠處的教堂飄來神聖的鐘聲，路旁樹叢上繽紛的樹葉散發出陣陣清香。這是一幅充滿了音樂感的畫作，只待你靜心聆聽。

In the rural area of Ukraine, the woman and children walk leisurely in the evening. They are quite peaceful and content under the company of the nature. The holy church bells from a distance and the colorful leaves of the tress on the roadside emitting refreshing fragrance, are injecting this painting with joy that can only be heard when you listen to it with peace.

黃昏｜油彩・畫布
Evening｜Oil on Canvas｜50x70cm｜2012

懷古風格的表現方式，有著端莊安詳面容的婦女，手捧著古老的水壺，優雅地向後凝盼。桌上的水果巧妙的提升了畫面的豐富性。

The painting depicts a nostalgic expression, whereas the woman with dignified and peaceful expression is holding an ancient pot, staring back in grace. The fruit on the table deliberately improves the abundance of the image.

拿著水罐的女子｜油彩·畫布
Lady with Jug｜Oil on Canvas｜60x80cm｜2012

烏克蘭初冬的天空是銀灰色的，地面鋪上了薄薄的一片白雪，枯黃的野草仍舊隱隱可見。啊！今年的第一場雪降下來了，意味著冬天的到來。

The sky of early winter in Ukraine is silver-gray color, whereas the ground is covered with a thin layer of snow and the yellow weeds can still be seen. This is the first snow this year and implies the coming of the winter.

又是冬至 │ 油彩·畫布
Winter Again │ Oil on Canvas │ 60x80cm │ 2012

信件對於人們具有著無盡的意義，那些經過再三斟酌之後一筆一劃寫下的字句，組成了飽含愛心的言語。郵差一程一程辛勞地傳遞，收信人焦急地打開信件時的喜悅……這些都是最寶貴的生活訊息，是人類記憶之鏈中的珍寶。

遺忘的信件｜油彩・畫布
Forgotten Letter｜Oil on Canvas｜75x50cm｜2012

純真無邪的女孩，宛如海芋般，潔白聖潔；這是畫家心目中最美麗的女孩。

The most beautiful girls in the mind of painters are innocent, naïve, pure, and holy like the Calla lilies.

(右圖)奇想之源-I｜油彩・畫布・壓克力顏料
(Right)Nests Chimeras - I｜Oil on Canvas, Acrylic ｜80x80cm｜ 2012

CHAPTER 6.

夢幻般的行旅。

—薩芬娜 *Safina Ksenia*

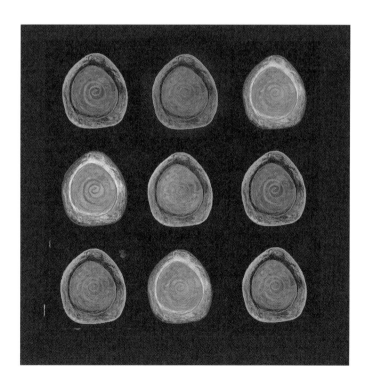

薩芬娜的父母是著名畫家，可想而知，她從小就受到濃濃的藝術薰陶。因之，她從藝的起點和品味大大超過了同代的畫家。她的繪畫從形式上來看，似乎屬於抽象繪畫範疇，但實際上卻不盡然。她的繪畫中隱藏著各種動植物、人物、古老的建築以及風景等等具體形象，只不過被作者大尺度的變形或誇張解體，並將其現實的形象淡化之後，又進行了重新組合。

正如畫家自敘，她所追求的是永恆的繪畫表現形式，也即是純粹的外在藝術表現樣式，她給觀眾的最深印象是色彩、肌理、筆觸，以及畫面的結構美感。她強調的是形式美，不過她的這種美感，正是蘇珊·朗格（Susanne K. Langer）倡導的「有意味的形式」。

薩芬娜對藝術追求執著，每一張畫的形式都是緊緊跟隨著主題而設定的。對待不同的主題，畫家會產生不同的情緒和感覺，也就創作出不同形式的畫作。她創作的內容極其豐富，有對大自然的讚頌、史詩的吟唱、神話的描述、歷史的陳說……等等。

她的作品深受波斯詩人，同時也是天文學家、數學家的歐瑪爾·海亞姆（Omar Khayyám）影響，同時還吸收了許多東方繪畫的表現方式，很自然地運用到她的畫作之中。她的畫，乍看起來，形式十分壯美，細細品來，其飽含哲理的內涵令人回味無窮。

除了內涵和純熟的技巧之外，她的作品非常純真。看她的畫，讓我想到《愛麗絲夢遊仙境》。觀者好像變成了愛麗絲，跳進山洞開啓了一趟神奇的探索之旅。這趟旅行也許是通往漫長歷史的行程，也許是走進了奇幻的神秘世界。觀者得以放下自我的主觀和框架，浸淫在薩芬娜所創造的清新感官王國裡。我相信，她的前途不可限量。

Safina's parents are famous painters. Obviously, she has been deeply influenced by art since she was a child. Therefore her career and taste of art are superior compared to her age and her peers. Her paintings seem to belong to the scope of abstract painting from the formality. However, they are not completely so. Her paintings are hidden with various animals, plants, figures, ancient architecture, and landscapes as well as other specific image. They are only deformed or dissembled by the author in large-scale of exaggeration, which lightens up the real image before undergoing re-structuring.

As the painter portrays, she pursuits the painting presentation and style of "eternity" ,which is purely the external artistic performing style. She impresses the audience the most with the colors, textures, brushes, and the structural aesthetics of images. She emphasizes on the beauty of forms. However, such aesthetics of her coincides with the "meaningful forms" advocated by Susanne K. Langer.

The form of each painting produced by Safina is designed closely with the theme. The painter tends to produce different emotions and feelings towards different themes, and thereby can create paintings of different formality. The content of her painting is quite rich with praises to the nature, the chanting for historical poem, portrait for myth, and narration for history.

Her works were deeply influenced by Omar Khayyám, the Persian poet, astronomer, and mathematician. What is valuable is the presentation of her absorption for many oriental paintings that are naturally incorporated into her paintings. Although her paintings look glamorous, they are in fact containing philosophical contexts that can make one ponder repeatedly.

In addition to the meaningful connotation and her mastery of skills, innocence can be seen in her works. Her works remind me of Alice in Wonderland. The viewers become Alice who jumped into the cave and experienced an amazing journey of discovery. The journey may lead the viewers to long past times or a fantastic mysterious world. During the journey, the viewers are given with the chance to put aside self-consciousness and subjective framework, bathing in the kingdom of fresh senses created by Safina. I can see the bright future of her.

亙古不變的日月，關照著安寧的鄉村大地，十字架高豎。這是烏克蘭凝聚的歷史寫照。

The sun and moon shining eternally above the tranquil rural land while the towering cross serve as the best reflection of the cohered history of Ukraine.

日月｜油彩‧畫布‧複合媒材
Day of the Moon｜
Oil on Canvas , Mixed Media｜60x80cm｜2012

簡單奇幻之物-I｜油彩‧畫布
Simple Magical Things - I｜Oil on Canvas｜80x60cm｜2012

畫家酷愛旅行，此畫從構圖和色彩都明顯受到古代波斯洞窟壁畫的影響，右邊經過石頭踏步通向的洞窟放置著東亞細亞人的雕像以及上部隱約出現的波斯風格穹頂建築，暗示了作品描繪的地域特色。暗紅色、灰綠色、黑灰色及白灰色、淺黃色的配置十分得當，畫面呈現出一種微微的靈光，神秘而溫暖，也帶有中國敦煌壁畫中早期被波斯文化影響過的畫風。這是作者被深深感動之後的再創作，美妙而深刻。

Safina enjoys traveling and this painting has been significantly affected by the ancient Persia cave murals from the composition and the colors. The right side shows the stone stairway towards the cave storing the sculpture of East Asians on the right and the Persian style of dome construction faintly from the top, implying the regional characteristics portrayed by the work. The dark red, gray-green, black-gray and white-gray colors are incorporated well with the light yellow color. The image presents a dim light that is mystic and warm with a painting style of the early Persian cultural influence in Chinese Dunhuang murals. This is a re-creation after the profound touching perceived by the author, which is both wonderful and profound.

雨｜油彩·畫布
Rain｜Oil on Canvas｜60x80cm｜2012

作品中出現了各種鎧甲、護心鏡、以及中世紀
的東西方武士，和人物、建築，被寓意著歷
史暴風般的混沌肌理掩飾著、吞噬著，向前流
動。畫作悲壯而大氣。

There are various armors, plastrons and
the oriental and western warriors from the
medieval ages, the figures, and buildings,
are concealed and devoured by the chaotic
context implying the storm of history, flowing
onward slowly. The painting is both tragic
and majestic.

作者以俯視的角度表現了一群在山石間奔命的野羊。牠們在雪地跑動，大片白色點綴著黑色山羊。灰色的山石化成符號，使得具象的形體變形為抽象的符號，強調出該作品形式的美感。

獵羊｜油彩・畫布・複合媒材

Hunting on Sheep｜Oil on Canvas , Mixed Media｜85x85cm｜2012

在石頭公園裡｜油彩·畫布
In the Garden of Stone｜Oil on Canvas｜50x45cm｜2012

典型的烏克蘭鄉村風景。多樣的拖擦筆觸製造成肌理，使單純色彩的畫面
變得非常豐富，令人產生無盡的遐想。

春天主題 | 油彩・畫布
Spring Motif | Oil on Canvas | 45x35cm | 2012

類似當代中國水墨畫的風格和佈局，採用平面構成的原理來安排黑白關係和色塊，作者巧妙地
將有肌理的色塊同平滑的區域穿插並置，使得畫面顯得活力盎然生機勃勃。淡綠色調籠罩著畫
面，加上星星點點的橙色金色色斑，寓意著初春的來臨。

春天｜油彩·畫布·粉蠟筆
Spring｜Oil on Canvas , Pastel｜60x80cm｜2012

韃靼人和他們的清真寺廟，遠處雪山白雪皚皚，寒冷的冰河似乎凝固，帶走了旅人的心。

The Tartars and their Mosque are located in remote mountains whereas white snow and cold glaciers seem to solidify and take away the heart of the travelers.

(左圖)部份藍色時光 | 油彩·畫布·壓克力顏料
(Left) Part of Blue Moments | Oil on Canvas , Acrylic | 35x80cm | 2012

(右圖)旅行-II | 油彩·畫布·壓克力顏料
(Right) Travel-II | Oil on Canvas , Acrylic | 55x40cm | 2012

(左圖)旅行-I｜油彩‧畫布‧壓克力顏料
(Left) Travel - I｜Oil on Canvas , Acrylic｜50x45cm｜2012

(右圖)旅行-III｜油彩‧畫布
(Right) Travel-III｜Oil on Canvas｜55x40cm｜2012

一位天真的孩子仰望著天空，鳥兒、大魚以及游動的魚群、房屋、樹彷彿都是孩子幻夢裡的
符號。象徵寓意手法。鳥和魚是薩芬娜作品中的固定造型符號。

郊外的花園，草舍、道路、樹木，開啓花園的鑰匙在女孩的心中。

The outskirt garden, cottage, roads, trees, and keys to the garden are in the mind of the girl.

(左圖)花園的魚群｜油彩·畫布·壓克力顏料
(Left) Fishes in the Garden｜Oil on Canvas , Acrylic｜80x60cm｜2011

(右圖)花園鑰匙｜油彩·畫布·壓克力顏料
(Right) Keys in the Garden｜Oil on Canvas , Acrylic｜65x60cm｜2010

素雅的版畫風格畫作：百合花盛開和凋落，美麗寧靜的時刻。

Simple and elegant engraving style paintings, the beautiful yet quiet moment of the blooming and withering lilies.

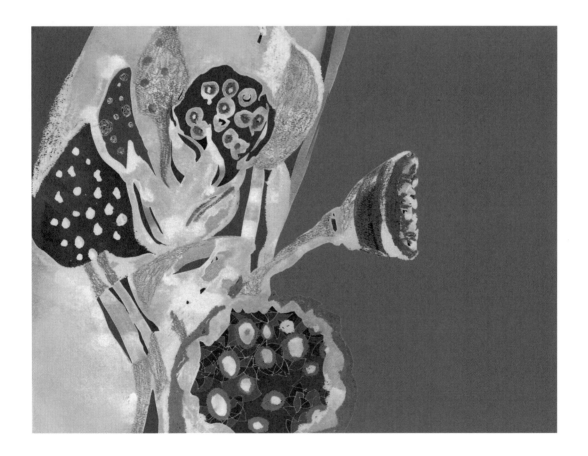

(左圖)百合花｜油彩‧畫布‧壓克力顏料
(Left) Lilies｜Oil on Canvas , Acrylic｜75x55cm｜2012

(右圖)奇想之源-II｜油彩‧畫布‧壓克力顏料
(Right) Nests Chimeras - II｜Oil on Canvas , Acrylic｜55x40cm｜2012

上升狀的教堂尖頂群在薄霧中隱現，似乎傳來了此起彼伏的祈禱鐘聲。

綠調子的肌理底色，使人聯想到敦煌壁畫。月夜，神秘的線刻小鳥像是岩壁畫。作
品有種淒楚的美，但是美得醉人。

搜尋奇幻之景｜油彩·畫布·壓克力顏料
Research Vision Thing Odd｜Oil on Canvas , Acrylic｜100x70cm｜2011

稚拙風格的男子帶著玉環，夢中情人在滿月裡。倒影般的男子是為著構圖的
對稱。這幅畫是一首情歌，也像是一首詩。

遊戲│油彩・畫布・壓克力顏料
Game │ Oil on Canvas , Acrylic │ 80x60cm │ 2011

當代東方抽象水墨淡彩風格，十分講究的平面構成技巧，體現了看似繁複無序，實質是經過多次推敲，精心佈局的純真美的再現。細看會有許多欣喜的發現，而魚圖形的反復出現，使畫面增加了趣味和動感。

奇想之源-III︱油彩‧畫布‧壓克力顏料

Nests chimeras - III︱Oil on Canvas , Acrylic︱130x100cm︱2012

史詩般的壁畫。東方旅者的深刻感受，對歷史的記錄和懷想。抽象的形式，現實的思想。

Epic murals, the profound feelings of the oriental travelers about the record and memory to the history. It's an abstract form with realistic thoughts.

簡單奇幻之物-II｜油彩·畫布
Simple Magical Things - II｜Oil on Canvas｜100x70cm｜2012

紛亂的建築物糾結在一起，霧靄中，灰色的空間喧鬧又空靈。到處布滿了十字架，好像聽到了教堂不安的鐘聲急促鳴響。一幅氣勢磅礴的歷史場面畫卷。

A magnificent historical scroll shows the chaotic buildings collaborated with one another, the gray space both bustling and empty in haze while if there are crosses everywhere with a remotely disturbing church bell sounds.

我的作品結合神話、民間傳說、怪誕及東方詩，並將它們反映在我的畫作上。我對於混合、熔化顏色的實驗很感興趣，將魚、鳥類與樹木交織在一起的圖像作品裡，說明它們在這個時間和空間中的經驗。在我的作品中，也以哲學的角度去探討人、時間及空間等關係，然而，作品中的語言之間的差異取決於心情、各種符號、煉金術及其他主題，顏色是不被清楚定義但具有象徵意義。

我反思神話的開始及神話寓言的解釋，這也是我對於創作的解決方案。我喜歡致力於自己的想法，並利用相片的類比進行美術的拼貼，將藝術作為傳遞的工具。

為了強調作品主題的永恆性，有些圖刻意缺乏具體特點，而畫作的組成也刻意不對稱。我所使用的媒材有油彩、綜合媒材、蝕刻及粉蠟筆，此外還有攝影和實驗性藝術，希望能透過畫面的多層次來闡述顏色。我期許在二次元的平面作品上創造出一個個的幻想世界，而這也是我一貫的方向。

– 薩芬娜自述 –

夜晚｜油彩·畫布
Night｜Oil on Canvas｜60x80cm｜2012

縱觀世界優秀繪畫，無論抽象或具象，無一不是凝聚了人文思想的精髓，並以此打動著觀眾的心靈。此次介紹的烏克蘭諸位畫家作品，幾乎都具備了以上所說的特質，與當代普遍流行的許多甚至是天價的時尚繪畫有著天壤之別的是，這些作品雖然大部分畫幅不大，但卻具有深刻的內涵。

這些畫家的作品清晰地表明，他們具備了良好的文化素養及廣泛的知識層面，涉及到了哲學、歷史、宗教、天文地理、神話傳說，甚至自然科學等諸多領域。因而其作品的價值遠遠超過了市場的定價，收藏價值的前景當屬久遠，更是值得分享的佳作。

書中列舉的幾位畫家風格多樣，他們的作品可以作為了解烏克蘭當代繪畫的窗口。

In view of the excellent paintings worldwide, regardless of abstract or specific, are all cohered with the essence of humanity and ideas that can move the spirit and soul of the audience. Nearly all the works produced by the Ukraine painters introduced this time are equipped with the aforementioned characteristics. They distinguish themselves from the many common, popular and even pricy fashionable painters in that although these works are not painted in large scale, they contain profound context.

They clearly express that these painters come with outstanding cultural temperament and wide range of knowledge. Their paintings involve philosophy, history, religion, geography and astronomy, myth and legends, and even multiple files such as natural science. Due to the value of their works far exceed the market price, the prospect of their collective value are quite optimistic and prolonged.

Painters listed in this book are with a variety of art styles. We believe that their works can be used as a small show window of the Ukrainian contemporary painting.

Index 附錄。

畫家簡歷

弗拉基米爾介紹。
VOLODYMYR NESKOROMNYI

弗拉基米爾‧涅斯柯羅姆內伊

1965年出生於烏克蘭的查布羅什地區，1985年畢業於第聶伯羅彼得羅夫斯克美術學院 ，隨後於1996年
完成在哈爾科夫工業美術大學的學業，專攻壁畫裝飾藝術。自1999年起，成為烏克蘭藝術家協會聯盟
的成員。海內外展覽紀錄多，作品獲海內外藏家收藏。

台灣展覽紀錄

2010　歌唱的白樺林-烏克蘭三位畫家聯展，美好時光畫廊，台灣台南

2011　浪漫樂章 - 烏克蘭當代藝術家聯展，新光三越百貨公司新天地館，台灣台南
　　　台北國際當代藝術博覽會，王朝酒店，台灣台北

2012　第一屆府城藝術博覽會，大億麗緻酒店，台灣台南
　　　人間萬象 - 弗拉基米爾個展，涵藝術空間，台灣台南

VOLODYMYR NESKOROMNYI

Born in 1965 at Zaporozhye region, Ukraine. In 1985 graduated from the Dnipropetrovsk Art College
named Vucetic. In 1996 graduated from the Kharkov Arts - Industrial Institute, Master Degree, in
major of "Monumental Decorative Art". From 1999, became member of National Union of Artists of
Ukraine. So far has been taking part in regional, republican and international exhibitions. Works are
private collected in Ukraine and abroad.

EXHIBITIONS IN TAIWAN

2010 - The Singing Birch Forest - Group Exhibition of three Ukrainian Artists, Wonderful
　　　Time Gallery, Tainan, Taiwan

2011 - Romantic Melody - Group Show of Ukrainian Artists, Mitsukoshi Department Store, Tainan,
　　　Taiwan

2011 - Young Art Taipei 2011, Sunworld Dynasty Hotel, Taipei, Taiwan

2012 - Hotel Art Fair in Fucheng, The Landis Hotel, Tainan, Taiwan

2012 - Kaleidoscope of Life - Volodymyr Solo Show, Han Art Space, Tainan, Taiwan

羅曼介紹。
ROMAN NOGIN

羅曼‧諾金

1976 年出生於烏克蘭的哈爾科夫市，1994年畢業於哈爾科夫國家藝術學院，主修劇場藝術。隨後於
1999 年完成在哈爾科夫國立設計與藝術學院的學業，專攻壁畫裝飾藝術，碩士學位。從2001年起，成
為烏克蘭藝術家青年協會聯盟的成員。

展覽

1996 烏克蘭-德國聯展FUNF+FUNF，COLLENHOF畫廊，德國紐倫堡

1997 烏克蘭-德國展覽SLIGHTLY，OPPOSITE畫廊，烏克蘭哈爾科夫

1999 列賓(Ilya Repin)155週年紀念展，烏克蘭哈爾科夫 / 秋天-99，烏克蘭基輔
　　　青年藝術家群展 NEW NAMES，烏克蘭哈爾科夫

2000 千禧年紀念耶穌聖誕特別展覽，烏克蘭哈爾科夫
　　　烏克蘭藝術節PRO ART，烏克蘭文化藝術中心，烏克蘭基輔

2001 藝術世界，美國紐約 / Fugro中心藝術展，美國德州休士頓
　　　藝術Fountainview Tower 展，美國德州休士頓 / Lyric Center藝術展，美國德州休士頓
　　　紐約藝術博覽會，美國紐約 / Wedge Tower 藝術展，美國德州休士頓
　　　哥倫比亞中心藝術展，美國德州休士頓 / Chase Tower 藝術展，美國德州休士頓
　　　加州藝術博覽會，美國加州舊金山 / 家與花園藝術展，美國德州休士頓
　　　家居與園藝展，美國德州休士頓 / 千禧年藝術展，美國德州休士頓

2002 康柏建築藝術展，美國德州休士頓 / 紐約藝術博覽會，美國紐約
　　　富國銀行廣場藝術展，美國德州休士頓 / One Westchase中心藝術展，美國德州休士頓
　　　二號入口藝術展，美國德州休士頓 / 美麗的房子藝術展，美國德州休士頓
　　　雪佛龍德士古大廈藝術展，美國德州休士頓

2005 個人畫展，藝術夥伴畫廊 (Art-Partners Gallery)，荷蘭鹿特丹

2006 現代藝術展覽，美國德州休士頓 / 爵士樂藝術展覽Jazz-Art，荷蘭鹿特丹

2007 爵士樂的藝術展覽 Jazz-Art，荷蘭鹿特丹

2008 現代藝術展覽，餅乾工廠畫廊 (The Biscuit Factory)，英國倫敦

2009 烏克蘭現代藝術節，烏克蘭文化藝術中心，烏克蘭基輔
　　　烏克蘭展，Fullbrigt美國中心，烏克蘭基輔

2010 從古至今歷史畫展覽，烏克蘭基輔
　　　歌唱的白樺林-烏克蘭三位畫家聯展，美好時光畫廊，台灣台南

2011 浪漫樂章-烏克蘭當代藝術家聯展，新光三越百貨公司新天地館，台灣台南
　　　台北國際當代藝術博覽會，王朝酒店，台灣台北
　　　美。正在進行曲 - 羅曼‧諾金個展，涵藝術空間，台灣高雄

2012 第一屆府城藝術博覽會，大億麗緻酒店，台灣台南
　　　璀璨二重唱 - 羅曼‧諾金／娜塔莎 雙個展，涵藝術空間，台灣台南
　　　台北國際當代藝術博覽會，喜來登大飯店，台灣台北
　　　台中藝術博覽會，長榮桂冠酒店，台灣台中
　　　流動的島嶼 - 羅曼‧諾金個展，涵藝術空間，台灣台南

ROMAN NOGIN

Born in city of Kharkov in 1976, finish the Kharkov State Art College in 1994, in major of " the Artist of Theatre ". Finish the Kharkov State Academy of Design and Arts in 1999, in major of " Monumental Decorative Art ". From 2001, became member of youth association of the Kharkov section of Union of the Artists of Ukraine.

EXHIBITIONS

1996 - Ukraines - German exhibition "Funf+Funf " gallery Collenhof, Nuremberg, Germany

1997 - Ukraines - German exhibition "Slightly" gallery Opposite, Kharkov, Ukraine

1999 - General - Ukrainian exhibition devoted 155 years of birth I.Repin, Kharkov, Ukraine

1999 - General - Ukrainian exhibition " Autumn - 99 ", Kiev, Ukraine

1999 - Exhibition of the young artists " New Names ", Kharkov, Ukraine

2000 - General - Ukrainian exhibition devoted 2000 of Christmas of the Christ, Kharkov, Ukraine

2000 - General Ukrainian festivals of arts " Pro Art ", The Ukrainian House, Kiev, Ukraine

2001 - Exhibition " Art of World ", New York, USA

2001 - Exhibition " Fugro Center Art Show ", Houston TX, USA

2001 - Exhibition " Fountainview Tower Art Show ", Houston TX, USA

2001 - Exhibition " Lyric Centre Art Show ", Houston TX, USA

2001 - Exhibition " New York Art Expo ", New York, USA

2001 - Exhibition " Wedge Tower Art Show ", Houston TX, USA

2001 - Exhibition " Columbia Center Art Show ", Houston TX, USA

2001 - Exhibition " Chase Tower Art Show ", Houston TX, USA

2001 - Exhibition " California Artexpo ", San Francisco CA, USA

2001 - Exhibition " Home and Garden Show ", Houston TX, USA

2001 - Exhibition " Millennium Art Show ", Houston TX, USA

2002 - Exhibition " Compaq Building Art Show ", Houston TX, USA

2002 - Exhibition " New York Art Expo ", New York, USA

2002 - Exhibition " Wells Fargo Plaza Art Show ", Houston TX, USA

2002 - Exhibition " One Westchase Center Art Show ", Houston TX, USA

2002 - Exhibition " Gateway II Art Show ", Houston TX, USA

2002 - Exhibition " House Beautiful Show ", Houston TX, USA

2002 - Exhibition " Texaco Chevron Tower Art Show ", Houston TX, USA

2005 - Solo Exhibition , gallery "Art-Partners", Rotterdam, Netherlands

2006 - Exhibition of modern art, Houston,USA

2006 - Exhibition a festival "Jazz-Art", Rotterdam,Netherlands

2007 - Exhibition a festival "Jazz-Art", Rotterdam,Netherlands

2008 - Exhibition of modern art, gallery " The Biscuit Factory ", London, Great Britain

2009 - General Ukrainian festivals of modern art, The Ukrainian House, Kiev, Ukraine

2009 - Exhibition in Ukraine - American centre of a name Fullbrigt, Kiev, Ukraine

2010 - Exhibition of historical painting " From an antiquity up to today ", Kiev, Ukraine

2010 - The Singing Birch Forest - Group Exhibition of three Ukrainian Artists, Wonderful Time Gallery, Tainan,Taiwan

2011 - Romantic Melody - Group Show of Ukrainian Artists, Mitsukoshi Department Store,Tainan, Taiwan

2011 - Young Art Taipei 2011, Sunworld Dynasty Hotel, Taipei, Taiwan

2011 - Beauty, Song of the Moment / Roman Nogin Solo Show, Han Art Space,Kaohsiung,Taiwan

2012 - Hotel Art Fair in Fucheng, The Landis Hotel, Tainan, Taiwan

2012 - The Duet of Brightness - Roman Nogin&Natasha Perekhodenko Show, Han Art Space,Tainan, Taiwan

2012 - Young Art Taipei 2012, Sherton Hotel, Taipei, Taiwan

2012 - T-Art 2012, Evergreen Laurel Hotel, Taichong,Taiwan

2012 - The Floating Islands-Roman Nogin Solo Show, Han Art Space, Tainan,Taiwan

娜塔莎介紹。
NATASHA PEREKHODENKO

娜塔莎‧別列克霍琴柯

1974 年出生於烏克蘭的盧甘斯克市，1994年畢業於盧甘斯克州藝術學院，專攻裝飾藝術。隨後於1999
年完成在哈爾科夫國立設計與藝術學院的學業，專攻壁畫裝飾藝術，碩士學位。從2001年起，成為
烏克蘭藝術家青年協會聯盟的成員。

展覽

1996 烏克蘭-德國聯展 FUNF+FUNF，COLLENHOF 畫廊，德國紐倫堡

1997 烏克蘭-德國展覽 SLIGHTLY，OPPOSITE 畫廊，烏克蘭哈爾科夫

1999 列賓(Ilya Repin)155週年紀念展，烏克蘭哈爾科夫 / 秋天-99，烏克蘭基輔
　　　青年藝術家群展 NEW NAMES，烏克蘭哈爾科夫

2000 千禧年紀念耶穌聖誕特別展覽，烏克蘭哈爾科夫
　　　烏克蘭藝術節PRO ART，烏克蘭文化藝術中心，烏克蘭基輔

2001 藝術世界，美國紐約 / Fugro 中心藝術展，美國德州休士頓
　　　藝術 Fountainview Tower 展 ，美國德州休士頓 / Lyric Center 藝術展 ，美國德州休士頓
　　　紐約藝術博覽會，美國紐約 / Wedge Tower 藝術展，美國德州休士頓
　　　哥倫比亞中心藝術展，美國德州休士頓 / Chase Tower 藝術展，美國德州休士頓
　　　加州藝術博覽會 ，美國加州舊金山 / 家與花園藝術展，美國德州休士頓
　　　家居與園藝展，美國德州休士頓 / 千禧年藝術展，美國德州休士頓

2002 康柏建築藝術展，美國德州休士頓 / 紐約藝術博覽會，美國紐約
　　　富國銀行廣場藝術展，美國德州休士頓 / One Westchase 中心藝術展，美國德州休士頓
　　　二號入口藝術展，美國德州休士頓 / 美麗的房子藝術展，美國德州休士頓
　　　雪佛龍德士古大廈藝術展 ，美國德州休士頓

2005 個人畫展，藝術夥伴畫廊 (Art-Partners Gallery) ，荷蘭鹿特丹

2006 現代藝術展覽，美國德州休士頓 / 爵士樂藝術展覽 Jazz-Art，荷蘭鹿特丹

2007 爵士樂的藝術展覽 Jazz-Art ，荷蘭鹿特丹

2008 現代藝術展覽，餅乾工廠畫廊 (The Biscuit Factory) ，英國倫敦

2009 烏克蘭現代藝術節，烏克蘭文化藝術中心，烏克蘭基輔
　　　烏克蘭展，Fullbrigt 美國中心，烏克蘭基輔

2010 歌唱的白樺林-烏克蘭三位畫家聯展，美好時光畫廊，台灣台南

2011 浪漫樂章-烏克蘭當代藝術家聯展，新光三越百貨公司新天地館，台灣台南
　　　台北國際當代藝術博覽會，王朝酒店，台灣台北

2012 第一屆府城藝術博覽會，大億麗緻酒店，台灣台南
　　　璀璨二重唱 - 羅曼‧諾金／娜塔莎 雙個展，涵藝術空間，台灣台南
　　　台北國際當代藝術博覽會，喜來登大飯店，台灣台北

NATASHA PEREKHODENKO

Born in city of Lugansk in 1974, finish the Lugansk State Art college in 1994, in major of " Decorative Art ". Finish the Kharkov State Academy of Design and Arts in 1999, in major of " Monumental Decorative Art ". From 2001, became member of youth association of the Kharkov section of Union of the Artists of Ukraine.

EXHIBITIONS

1996 - Ukraines - German exhibition "Funf+Funf" gallery Collenhof, Nuremberg, Germany

1997 - Ukraines - German exhibition "Slightly" gallery Opposite, Kharkov, Ukraine

1999 - General - Ukrainian exhibition devoted 155 years of birth I.Repin, Kharkov, Ukraine

1999 - General - Ukrainian exhibition " Autumn - 99 ", Kiev, Ukraine

1999 - Exhibition of the young artists " New Names ", Kharkov, Ukraine

2000 - General - Ukrainian exhibition devoted 2000 of Christmas of the Christ, Kharkov, Ukraine

2000 - General Ukrainian festivals of arts " Pro Art ", The Ukrainian House, Kiev, Ukraine

2001 - Exhibition " Art of World ", New York, USA

2001 - Exhibition " Fugro Center Art Show ", Houston TX, USA

2001 - Exhibition " Fountainview Tower Art Show ", Houston TX, USA

2001 - Exhibition " Lyric Centre Art Show ", Houston TX, USA

2001 - Exhibition " New York Art Expo ", New York, USA

2001 - Exhibition " Wedge Tower Art Show ", Houston TX, USA

2001 - Exhibition " Columbia Center Art Show ", Houston TX, USA

2001 - Exhibition " Chase Tower Art Show ", Houston TX, USA

2001 - Exhibition " California Artexpo ", San Francisco CA, USA

2001 - Exhibition " Home and Garden Show ", Houston TX, USA

2001 - Exhibition " Millennium Art Show ", Houston TX, USA

2002 - Exhibition " Compaq Building Art Show ", Houston TX, USA

2002 - Exhibition " New York Art Expo ", New York, USA

2002 - Exhibition " Wells Fargo Plaza Art Show ", Houston TX, USA

2002 - Exhibition " One Westchase Center Art Show ", Houston TX, USA

2002 - Exhibition " Gateway II Art Show ", Houston TX, USA

2002 - Exhibition " House Beautiful Show ", Houston TX, USA

2002 - Exhibition " Texaco Chevron Tower Art Show ", Houston TX, USA

2005 - Solo Exhibition , gallery "Art-Partners", Rotterdam, Netherlands

2006 - Exhibition of modern art, Houston,USA

2006 - Exhibition a festival "Jazz-Art", Rotterdam,Netherlands

2007 - Exhibition a festival "Jazz-Art", Rotterdam,Netherlands

2008 - Exhibition of modern art, gallery " The Biscuit Factory ", London, Great Britain

2009 - General Ukrainian festivals of modern art, The Ukrainian House, Kiev, Ukraine

2009 - Exhibition in Ukraine - American centre of a name Fullbrigt, Kiev, Ukraine

2010 - The Singing Birch Forest - Group Exhibition of three Ukrainian Artists, Wonderful Time Gallery, Tainan,Taiwan

2011 - Romantic Melody - Group Show of Ukrainian Artists, Mitsukoshi Department Store,Tainan, Taiwan

2011 - Young Art Taipei 2011, Sunworld Dynasty Hotel, Taipei, Taiwan

2012 - Hotel Art Fair in Fucheng, The Landis Hotel, Tainan, Taiwan

2012 - The Duet of Brightness-Roman Nogin&Natasha Perekhodenko Show, Han Art Space,Tainan, Taiwan

2012 - Young Art Taipei 2012, Sherton Hotel, Taipei, Taiwan

亞歷克山大介紹。

ALEXANDER SERDYUK

亞歷克山大 · 謝爾都烏克

1982 年出生於烏克蘭的哈爾科夫市，1994年畢業於哈爾科夫國家藝術學院，主修劇場藝術。隨後於 2008 年完成在哈爾科夫國立設計與藝術學院的學業，專攻壁畫裝飾藝術，碩士學位。從2010年起，成為烏克蘭藝術家協會聯盟的成員。

展覽

1999 烏克蘭藝術家日，烏克蘭基輔

2000 烏克蘭勝利的55年，烏克蘭基輔 / 烏克蘭新銳藝術家展覽，烏克蘭基輔
　　　獨特的烏克蘭，烏克蘭基輔 / 烏克蘭 藝術家日，烏克蘭基輔

2001 聖誕節展覽，烏克蘭哈爾科夫 / 烏克蘭 藝術家日，烏克蘭基輔

2002 畢業製作，烏克蘭利沃夫

2003 烏克蘭年輕氣息 - 獨特的烏克蘭，烏克蘭利沃夫 / 烏克蘭 - 藝術家日，烏克蘭基輔

2004 亞歷克山大 · 謝爾都烏克個展，哈爾科夫藝術博物館， 烏克蘭哈爾科夫
　　　烏克蘭藝術家日，烏克蘭基輔

2005 獨特的烏克蘭，烏克蘭基洛夫勒德

2006 獨特的烏克蘭，烏克蘭敖德薩 / 烏克蘭當代藝術家，烏克蘭基輔
　　　大師與學生，AVEK畫廊，烏克蘭哈爾科夫

2007 烏克蘭聖誕節展覽，烏克蘭基輔 / 獨特的烏克蘭，烏克蘭基輔
　　　烏克蘭年輕藝術家展覽，烏克蘭哈爾科夫 / 烏克蘭草原，烏克蘭
　　　哈爾科夫國家設計與藝術 - 不朽的繪畫展，AVEK畫廊， 烏克蘭哈爾科夫

2008 亞歷克山大 · 謝爾都烏克個展，基輔-哈爾科夫捷運車站36藝廊， 烏克蘭基輔
　　　亞歷克山大 · 謝爾都烏克個展，基輔理工學院，烏克蘭基輔
　　　亞歷克山大 · 謝爾都烏克個展，人文學苑，烏克蘭基輔
　　　烏克蘭當代藝術家雙年展，烏克蘭基輔、利沃夫、烏日哥羅德
　　　援助孤兒拍賣會展覽，依萬高博物館，烏克蘭基輔

2009 亞歷克山大 · 謝爾都烏克個展，紐倫堡樓， 烏克蘭哈爾科夫
　　　亞歷克山大 · 謝爾都烏克個展，市立美術館， 烏克蘭哈爾科夫
　　　烏克蘭與世界展覽 - Nikolay Gogol，烏克蘭波爾塔瓦 / 五位烏克蘭藝術家的詮釋，烏克蘭加拿大中心， 加拿大多倫多 / Yard Handwerkerhof Masters 展覽，德國紐倫堡

2010 五位烏克蘭藝術家的詮釋，捷克布拉格

2011 亞歷克山大 · 謝爾都烏克個展，烏克蘭蘇米
　　　烏克蘭女性畫展，烏克蘭基輔 / 獨特的烏克蘭，烏克蘭基輔
　　　烏克蘭的禮物，烏克蘭基輔

2012 烏克蘭聖誕節展覽，烏克蘭基輔 / 烏克蘭當代藝術家雙年展，烏克蘭基輔
　　　台北國際當代藝術博覽會，喜來登大飯店，台灣台北
　　　夢幻般的詩境 - 亞歷克山大 · 謝爾都烏克個展，涵藝術空間，台灣台南

ALEXANDER SERDYUK

Born in city of Kharkov in 1982, graduated from Kharkov Art school with honors in 2002, finished Kharkov State Academy of Design and Arts, Department of Monumental painting in 2008 with defended a diploma in the specialty " Monumental Decorative Art ", obtained Masters degree. Since 2008 have been working as a Teacher of drawing, Department of drawing in Kharkov State Academy of Design and Arts. From 2010, became member of the National Union of Artists of Ukraine. Awarded by a silver medal of the Academy of Arts of Ukraine for the work " Kobzars Tale " in 2010.

EXHIBITIONS

1999 - Ukrainian " Artist's Day ", Kiev, Ukraine

2000 - Ukrainian "55 Years of Victory", Kiev, Ukraine

2000 - Ukrainian Youth's Exhibition, Kiev, Ukraine

2000 - Exhibition " Picturesque Ukraine ", Kiev, Ukraine

2000 - Ukrainian " Artist's Day ", Kiev, Ukraine

2001 - Ukrainian Christmas exhibition, Kharkov, Ukraine

2001 - Ukrainian " Artist's Day ", Kiev, Ukraine

2002 - Diploma Works' Exhibition, Lviv, Ukraine

2003 - Ukrainian Youth Plein Air " Picturesque Ukraine " in Lviv, Ukraine

2003 - Ukrainian " Artist's Day ", Kiev, Ukraine

2004 - Exhibition in Kharkov Art Museum(32 graphic works), Kharkov, Ukraine
       Ukrainian " Artist's Day ", Kiev, Ukraine

2005 - Ukrainian " Picturesque Ukraine ", Kirovograd, Ukraine

2006 - Ukrainian " Picturesque Ukraine ", Odessa, Ukraine

2006 - Biennial of Ukrainian Historical Painting " From Tripilya Till Nowadays in the
       Images of Contemporary Artists ", Kiev, Ukraine

2006 - Exhibition " Maestro and his students ", gallery AVEK, Kharkov, Ukraine

2007 - Ukrainian Christmas exhibition, Kiev, Ukraine

2007 - Ukrainian " Picturesque Ukraine ", Kiev, Ukraine

2007 - Ukrainian Youth's Exhibition, Kharkov, Ukraine

2007 - International Symposium of Stone Sculpture and Painting " Ukrainian steppe ",
       Svyatogorsk, Ukraine

2007 - Exhibition " Kharkov National Academy of Design and Arts, Monumental Painting
        " gallery VEK, Kharkov, Ukraine

2008 - Exhibition " Kiev-Kharkov express ", Gallery 36, Kiev, Ukraine

2008 - Exhibition in Kiev Polytechnic Institute, Kiev, Ukraine

2008 - Exhibition in Humanities lyceum, Kiev, Ukraine

2008 - Biennial of Ukrainian Historical Painting "From "Tripilya" Till Nowadays in the
        Images of Contemporary Artists ", Kiev - Lviv - Uzhgorod, Ukraine

2008 - Exhibition and Auction in aid of orphans, Ivan Gonchar Museum, Kiev, Ukraine

2009 - Exhibition " The land where I live ", Nuremberg House, Kharkov, Ukraine

2009 - Exhibition " Maestro and student ", Municipal Gallery, Kharkov, Ukraine

2009 - Ukrainian Exhibition " Nikolay Gogol, Ukraine and the World ", Poltava, Ukraine

2009 - Exhibition " Five Interpretations of Ukraine " Ukrainian - Canadian center, Toronto, Canada

2009 - Exhibition Hall " Masters' Yard Handwerkerhof ", Nuremberg, Germany

2010 - Exhibition " Five Interpretations of Ukraine", Prague, Czech Republic

2011 - Exhibition " Two Serdiuks ", Sumi, Ukraine

2011 - Ukrainian Exhibition " Ukrainian Women ", Kiev, Ukraine

2011 - Ukrainian Exhibition " Picturesque Ukraine ", Kiev, Ukraine

2011 - Ukrainian Exhibition " Ukrainian Gifts ", Kiev, Ukraine

2012 - Ukrainian Christmas exhibition, Kiev, Ukraine

2012 - Biennial of Ukrainian Historical Painting " From Tripilya " Till Nowadays in the
       Images of Contemporary Artists ", Kiev, Ukraine

2012 - Young Art Taipei 2012, Sunworld Dynasty Hotel, Taipei, Taiwan

2012 - Exhibition " The Fantastic Poetry ", Han Art Space, Tainan, Taiwan

薩芬娜介紹。
SAFINA KSENIA

薩芬娜‧克謝妮亞

1988年出生於烏克蘭，2009年畢業於哈爾科夫國立設計與藝術學院平面藝術系，學士學位。2008年入選為烏克蘭藝術家青年協會聯盟成員。2011年完成哈爾科夫國立設計與藝術學院的學業，專攻平面藝術，碩士學位。2012年入選為烏克蘭全國藝術家聯盟成員。

展覽
2005 平面繪畫展覽競賽，匈牙利
2006 烏克蘭全國藝術家聯盟聖誕聯展，烏克蘭哈爾柯夫
2007 平面藝術展，烏克蘭文化中心，俄羅斯莫斯科
2008 迷宮文明，烏克蘭辛菲羅波爾
2009 迷你Cadaqués 繪畫展， 西班牙巴塞隆納 / 紐倫堡聖誕聯展，烏克蘭哈爾柯夫
　　　東方聯展，俄羅斯彼得堡
2010 烏克蘭全國藝術家聯盟繪畫展覽競賽，烏克蘭基輔 / 繪畫展，斯多利夫、蒙特內哥羅
2011 繪畫Premio Acqui展， 義大利亞歷山德里亞
　　　寇斯尤里斯基小巷展覽，接觸藝廊， 烏克蘭哈爾柯夫
　　　伯斯坦諾卡活動，俄羅斯葉卡捷琳
2012 平面藝術三年展，烏克蘭全國藝術家聯盟，烏克蘭基輔
　　　馬拉維奇獎，藝術家中心，俄羅斯莫斯科
　　　旋律美，當代藝術慕尼黑 – 基輔研究中心，烏克蘭基輔
　　　夢幻行旅 – 薩芬娜個展，涵藝術空間，台灣台南

SAFINA KSENIA

Born in city of Kharkov in 1988, finish the Kharkov State Academy of Design and Arts in 2009, in major of " Graphics ". Finish the Kharkov State Academy of Design and Arts in 2011, in major of " Graphics ". From 2008 - became member of youth association of the Kharkov section of Union of the Artists of Ukraine. From 2012 - became member of the National Union of Artists of Ukraine.

EXHIBITIONS

2005 - Competition Exhibition graphics, Hungary
2006 - Christmas Exhibition National Union of Artists of Ukraine, Kharkov, Ukraine
2007 - Exhibition graphics, Cultural center of Ukraine, Moscow, Russia
2008 - Labyrinths of civilization, Simferopol, Ukraine
2009 - Mini Print International of Cadaqués, Barcelona, Spain
2009 - Christmas Exhibition, House Nuremberg, Kharkov, Ukraine
2009 - Orienting, St. Petersburg, Russia
2010 - Competition Exhibition graphics, National Union of Artists of Ukraine, Kiev, Ukraine
2010 - Exhibition painting, Stoliv, Montenegro
2011 - Premio Acqui, Exhibition graphics, Italy
2011 - Project Postanovka, Ekaterinburg, Russia
2011 - Contact, Gallery Kostyurinsky alley, Exhibition painting, Kharkov, Ukraine
2012 - Triennial exhibition of graphics, National Union of Artists of Ukraine, Kiev, Ukraine
2012 - Award Malevich, Central House of Artists, Moscow, Russia
2012 - München - Kiev Institute of Contemporary Art " Rhythm Section "
2012 - Dreamlike Journey - Safina Ksenia Solo Show, Han Art Space, Tainan, Taiwan

作者介紹

林暄涵

藝術經紀人。涵藝術經紀公司執行長。致力於推廣國際當代藝術。重視藝術品深層的內涵,追求藝術的純粹性,引介帶給心靈永恆平靜的藝術品。著作:《雲端上的歌者》、繪本《外婆,蝸牛來了!》。

作者｜林暄涵　　文字顧問｜岑龍　　編輯｜涵藝術經紀公司　　美術設計｜邱鈺喬　　英文翻譯｜哈佛翻譯社　　出版｜讀家文化出版有限公司
地址｜802 高雄市苓雅區光華一路 241 號 5F 之 5　　電話｜07-2234055　　傳真｜07-2231636　　信箱｜readersbook@yahoo.com.tw
讀家網站｜www.reader5212.com　　涵藝術網站｜www.hanartspace.com　　初版一刷｜2012 年 11 月 7 日
經銷商｜貿騰發賣股份有限公司　　地址｜新北市中和區中正路 880 號 14 樓　　電話｜02-8227-5988　　傳真｜02-8227-5989　　網站｜www.namode.com

ISBN　978-986-5902-02-5（平裝）　　版權所有 ・ 翻印必究